I0555823

# THE GATE TO OBLIVION

## TEMPORAL ARMISTICE BOOK 3

### MATTHEW S. COX

DIVISION ZERO PRESS

The Gate to Oblivion

Temporal Armistice Book 3

© 2018 Matthew S. Cox

Cover by Alexandria Thompson (www.gothic-fate.com)

ISBN (eBook): 978-1-949174-86-1

ISBN (Print): 978-1-949174-87-8

# CONTENTS

# 1

## TABLE MANNERS

Frustrated at dying for the sixty-billionth time, I succumb to the rage of a thousand burning hells and cry out in anguish across the cosmos. May the halls of the ancient elder gods tremble at my wrath… or, uhh, something like that.

I draw my arm back to hurl the controller, but stop myself. I'm not really mad at the PlayStation as much as sick with worry over destroying the world. I don't wanna do it.

The *real* world that is, not the PlayStation one.

Suppose the only *good* thing that would accomplish is finally bringing an end to people quibbling over if Pluto should be a planet or not. And, yeah, throwing the controller's a bad idea, too. For one thing, I don't want to drop fifty bucks on a new one. For another, I might hurt someone in the next apartment.

Other than being stuck between two warring factions of extraplanar beings, I had been in a pretty good mood tonight before the game got me pissed off. It's Saturday and I'm not on the swing shift this week. Had a lunch date with Jason earlier, and I plan to spend most of tomorrow with him. The advantage to working twelve-hour shifts is constant three-day weekends—except for when I have to cover Saturday-Sunday once a month.

And honestly, that's mostly a formality. They just want some people at the stationhouse in case someone shows up there needing help. We're all basically on duty all the time. Again, not that I mind. If I did, I wouldn't have taken the job.

With a sigh, I revert to my last save game in *Fractured: The Endless Waste*, and once again attempt to make it through the 'reaper's gauntlet.' It's a barren area of white sand with these teepee-shaped piles of bone here and there that don't offer much cover. Between land mines, snipers at the distant raider fortress, and these mutant pygmy things... ugh. As much as I like this game, it's about at a point where I put it down for a few weeks.

My front door clicks and creaks open. Either I'm about to be robbed or that's the neighbor kid. I've wound up watching her for her mother so often, I gave her a key. Well, that's mostly so she can get in here if she needs a safe place. Not that I don't trust her mother—I don't trust her taste in guys.

"Brook?" calls Ashley.

"Yeah."

"You naked?" asks Ashley.

I glance down at my sweat pants and tank top. "Nope."

"Cool." The front door shuts. Seconds later, my eight-year-old neighbor walks around the end of the couch. She's barefoot and wearing an adult-sized black T-shirt for a dress. The cartoon kitten on it has one paw raised, a single blade-like claw popped out despite huge eyes and an adorable expression. The caption 'I may be cute but I will cut you' wraps around the cat in fancy, girly writing. Her enchanted faerie doll, purple wings aglow, hovers beside her.

I pause the game and chuckle at her.

"All my stuff's in bags. It's laundry day. This is mom's shirt." She plops down on the sofa next to me, then lands the faerie on the coffee table before rubbing the control ring to make it 'sleep' "Does taking your clothes off make magic stronger?"

I cough. "What? Where'd you get that from?"

She swings her feet back and forth, gazing at the character on the TV. "Onna internet. Found a page with spells. Couldn't read it, but the lady in the pictures didn't have anything on but runes painted on her. Ooh. What game is that?"

"What are you doing reading about spells? Umm. I don't really know that much about magic." I blink. Of course, now part of me has an urge to find out if there is any truth to that or if the artist just wanted to be racy. "And this is a game for grown-ups."

Ashley sticks her tongue out at me, then laughs. "'Cause. A responsible demon summoner uses magic on their minions to make them tougher and keep them happy."

I can't quite bring myself to say I'm not her minion. Before a response comes to mind, someone knocks. After saving/exiting the game, I return to the menu and hand her the controller on my way to the door.

Tracy—Ashley's mother—smiles at me when I open it. She's struggling to hold up two overfilled laundry baskets and her backpack of books. "Hey. Thanks again for watching her. I hate to ask, but is there any chance you could head down to the laundry room in like forty minutes and move our shit to the dryer?"

"Yeah, sure. Someone will throw it on the floor if it sits too long."

"Cool." She struggles to set the baskets down and hands me a little plastic baggie with quarters in it. "For the dryer."

"'Kay. What time are you coming back?"

She looks at her phone to check the time. "Class is over at ten, so I should be back here around 10:30 to 10:45."

Ashley zooms over and hugs her mother. "Bye, Mom. Have fun at *school.*"

The kid has way too much fun saying that.

"Don't give Brook a hard time, okay? Stay safe."

"I won't." Ashley folds her arms. "My minion will protect me."

Tracy picks the baskets back up and trudges off to the stairwell. The kid and I relocate to the couch and proceed to play a child-friendly racing game with oversized cartoon animals: *The Fast and the Furry-ous.* Whoever labeled it with 'mild cartoon violence' has a rather strange definition of the word 'mild.'

Within a few minutes, I pick up that Ashley's being unusually quiet. I look at her and get a sense she's worried.

"Something bothering you?"

She turns her entire body with the effort of steering her cartoon weasel around a corner. "Yeah."

"Want to talk about it?"

Ashley considers for a moment before nodding. "Mom was on the phone with a man, sorta arguing. She kept saying stuff like she can't do that shit anymore. Or that shit is crazy and she left that life behind."

Hmm. That doesn't sound good, but at least she said no. "Was she afraid?"

"Nah." She shrugs. "Not really. Mom sounded more like me when she tells me to clean my room and I don't wanna."

That gets me to chuckle. "Any idea who that was?"

"She called him F-bomb."

I furrow my eyebrows. "Did she call him that word, or literally 'F-bomb?'"

"She didn't call him 'literally f-bomb.' She called him F-bomb."

"The guy's name is fuck?"

Ashley rolls her eyes then shoots me an 'are you an idiot?' stare. "No. His name is 'F-bomb.' Eff-dash-bomb."

"Got it." I sigh at myself. "I really should stop using that language around you. Can't help it."

"It's who you are." She grins, then pretend whispers, "Besides. I've heard 'em all from Mom. You're not corrupting me."

"Hah!"

The instant I throw my head back to laugh, she unpauses the game. Ooh! Brat! I refocus on my little car as fast as I can, narrowly avoiding going off the track and crashing. No idea what it is about certain types of games, but it seems like whenever we play one made for little kids, she wins more often than not. And no, I'm not letting her. Guess I'm overthinking trying to slow down on turns or something and the game isn't complicated enough for that to matter.

Ashley's stomach growls.

I glance sideways at her on a straightaway. She's sunk into the cushions enough that her shirt looks almost flat. The kid is so damn skinny I've basically got an empty T-shirt draped over the sofa next to me. Guess Tracy ran out of Starbucks throw-outs again. Fair bet she didn't eat much before her mother left to catch her 7 p.m. class. Ugh. I remember how much it sucked to work constantly while going to college. Only I did it in the reverse: day school with a night job.

Ashley's little go-kart zooms over the finish line a second and change before mine. She thrusts both arms straight up and cheers.

"You only won because you unpaused it when I wasn't looking." I stick my tongue out at her.

She giggles. "You've been playing video games longer than I'm old. I need every advantage."

"Heh. You're going to be a lawyer when you grow up."

Ashley gives me a blank look.

I expect a crack about how she'll stick to summoning demons because it's less evil, but then I remember she's only eight.

Her confusion shifts to mild awkwardness. She bites her lip and twists the controller around in her hands. "Can I have some food, please?"

"Sure. And you don't need to be ashamed of asking."

She nods. "I 'member you told me it's okay to ask. Saw you look at me when my tummy yelled."

"C'mon." I ruffle her hair, then lead the way to the kitchen.

Hmm. I hate standing by an open freezer. Too damn cold. So, I grab the first box that catches my eye and hold up a frozen chicken pot pie. Ashley shrugs with a 'that'll work' expression. Geez, poor kid. Eight-year-olds should not be willing to eat whatever lands in front of them purely because it's food.

Then again, I know how she feels. During the 'Saltine weeks' when I was a kid, this pot pie would've been like filet mignon. After unboxing it, I pop it in the rune oven and hit the red gem. Thin strands of purple lightning crackle around inside the chamber. In a few seconds, the fragrance of chicken and gravy fills the kitchen.

"Whew." Ashley emerges from under the table. "It smells right."

"My oven isn't *that* bad."

She blinks up at me. "Umm... yeah it is. Hot dogs aren't s'posed to *explode.*"

We sit around in the kitchen for a bit while Ashley tells me about her faerie, Vy. (The toy my friend Natalie made.) Apparently, she used to be Princess Violet, but her parents died to an assassin so she's here in Philly to hide.

"Are there real faeries?" asks Ashley.

"Yep. Though they don't come into the city. They *hate* technology. It scares them the same way alarm clocks ward me off."

She giggles.

*Chime.*

"Oh, crap," whispers Ashley. "You forgot to say the Words of Protection."

I sigh and get up. "It still smells like chicken pot pie. You know, sometimes, this rune oven works."

Nothing appears out of the ordinary when I open the door. The formerly-frozen pot pie sits at the middle of the rune oven looking all innocent and delicious. A bit of steam rises out of the three neat holes at the center, and it doesn't smell like it's undergone flavor reassignment surgery.

Out of habit, I grab oven mitts. Ashley bursts into laughter. What? Oh. Duh. I toss the gloves and grab the thing with my bare hands. It doesn't even feel warm to me. After setting it on a plate for her and grabbing a fork, I sit catty-corner at the table.

Ashley picks up the fork and points it at the pot pie as if threatening it to behave. The poor kid's practically drooling at the smell. She jams the fork right in the middle, a look of wide-eyed eagerness on her face.

Her expression shifts to alarm.

The fork wobbles.

A tiny growl emanates from the pot pie.

She *eeps* and leans back, abandoning the fork—which continues sticking straight up from the middle of the crust. When the fork begins to rise, she glares at it, then me. "You said something about your rune oven *not* sucking?"

The crust bursts in a spray of beige gravy and carrot bits, revealing a tiny humanoid figure that resembles a demonic infant with an oversized head and tiny needle teeth. Two pointy carrots stick out like horns, and the thing is either covered in gravy or is made out of it. A three-way-staredown lasts all of two seconds before the critter flings itself at the child's face.

Ashley screams loud enough to hurt my ears and dives out of her chair.

Vestigial wings fluttering, the little horror sails across my kitchen and hits the cabinet doors with a *splat.* It leaves a blot of gravy (and small claw marks) as it slides to the floor. Ashley rolls back to her feet and grabs the fork, taking on the stance of a fencer. Unfazed by her 'weapon,' the critter charges.

Her confidence breaks. She runs in circles around the table screaming, the pot-pie demon in close pursuit. I can't quite tell if the thing is actually dangerous or only bizarre. It eventually stops going *around* the table and cuts under it, jumping onto her leg. She shrieks.

"Ow! It's hot!"

The small demon rears back to bite her. Ashley swats it away before its teeth make contact.

"Stop playing with your food," I say.

She hops up onto the table, whining and rubbing her leg. "My food is trying to eat *me!*"

Unable to reach Ashley from the floor, the ten-inch-tall thing zips over and bites me on the shin. Ow. Bastard. It's got real teeth. I go to grab it, but it leaps away. Guess it's my turn to chase it around. It scrambles back and forth across the kitchen, pausing under the table to give me the finger since it thinks I'm too tall to follow it under there.

I dive.

It zooms aside, leaving me sliding on my chest. Fortunately, I come to a halt before my head makes contact with the wall.

Sigh.

I prop my chin on my hand and tap my claws on the linoleum for a few seconds. When it starts coming up behind me, I briefly entertain the idea of letting my tail out—but I don't want to ruin these sweat pants. It screams when I fling myself over into a seated position and grab for it. Goopy pot pie stew oozes between my fingers. The creature slips from my grasp and scurries back across the kitchen, laughing at me.

Well, that answers the question. It *isn't* solid. I lick my palm. Yep. Still tastes like chicken pot pie.

It climbs the table leg.

Ashley scoots back as it pulls itself onto the table surface. "Banish it! It's gonna eat me!"

"Which plane of hell contains the frozen food aisle?" I ask.

Her eyes radiate terror, but she puts on her best angry face and makes a fist at it. Undeterred, the imp raises its hands, claws out, and runs across the table at her.

I leap at it, but the little bastard zooms out of the way. I come down atop my kitchen table like a bad Eighties wrestler, slide over it, flip, and land flat on my back on the floor.

"Ow."

A soft *splat* comes from above me.

The demon sails off the table, hits the wall above the sink, and falls in.

"Ow!" shouts Ashley. "It's still hot!"

Okay, I'm a dumbass. I'm trying to chase this stupid thing around physically. The instant I see it creeping over the edge of the sink, I seize it in a telekinetic grip. Tiny arms and legs blur into a frenzy of motion, flailing desperately for purchase on anything solid. With it contained, I ease myself upright. Ashley's still standing on the table, her right foot in the air, covered to the ankle in gravy.

I force the little horror into the disposer sink. Gurgling and screaming, it vanishes out of sight under the rubber gasket. Another telekinetic tweak hits the switch, setting off a geyser of beige goo, peas, and carrots that splatters on the ceiling. I stare at the dripping glop, shaking my head.

"Okay, that's totally fubar. How the hell did six gallons of this shit come out of a tiny aluminum bowl?"

"Napkin please," says Ashley.

I start to reach for the paper towels, but freeze still as another little imp-shape rises out of the goop.

"Oh, screw you." I sprout my claws and grab the thing, impaling it on five onyx blades.

That time, it emits an agonized wail, solidifies in my hand, and goes limp. Okay, now this is super disgusting. It feels like I'm holding a lump of ground beef. It looks like a dead baby, and it still smells like chicken pot pie.

I drop it in the sink with a *splut* and glance at Ashley.

We stare at each other for two seconds before both of us say, "Pizza," at the same time.

"Good call." I swipe a paper towel from the roll.

"Dude…" Ashley grabs my shoulders for balance as I wipe off her foot. "You need a new rune oven. This one's like cursed or something."

Laughing, I grasp her under the arms and set her back on the floor. "Yeah… But it's not actually mine. It's the apartment's."

"Oh. Guess that's why Mom never uses ours."

"C'mon. Time to go move your laundry to the dryer. Then I'll order a pizza."

Right as I start out of the kitchen, I catch the faint echo of a small growl coming from the kitchen sink.

Son of a bitch.

# 2

## NATURAL DISASTER

Well, the little horror never came back.

Assuming I didn't imagine that growl, someone else somewhere else is going to have an unusual experience. Hopefully, it doesn't climb up out of someone's toilet. Anyway, the rest of the night went by in a haze of pizza and video games. Ashley passed out before her mother returned at a little after eleven due to traffic.

Sunday, I'm free.

Free from work as well as babysitting responsibilities.

Jason shows up around ten and we wind up killing a few hours at the Arcanist's Museum. The place really is aimed more at kids, but I made the mistake of saying I'd never been there and he insisted. Okay, I admit it makes for a cute date. Mostly, it's got all these 'how does magic work' type exhibits with a liberal helping of hands-on fun-to-play-with stuff. And the history stuff is cool. Like how they needed eldritch rods on trains back in the Old West so thunderbirds didn't destroy them. Those things *still* sometimes attack trains or cars. Fortunately, the establishment of portals in most major cities eliminated the need for trains. Why sit for hours in an uncomfortable seat when going from New York to Los Angeles by portal takes seconds? Okay, cost... yeah I get that. The mages who run the portal network are greedy.

Speaking of travel, another exhibit shows some stuff about an attempt to create flying machines for passenger travel. Some dude named Sikorsky in Russia fiddled around with them in 1914, but a lovesick dragon mistook the thing he made for a female and... well. Yeah. Kinda gives new meaning to 'crash and burn' on a date. No one dared attempting passenger air travel in the States. The thunderbirds are still too angry over the whole displacement of the indigenous population. Small things like helicopters or enchanted cars are reasonably safe. But anything big enough to carry passengers on a commercial scale... yeah. Considering the portal network, it wouldn't be worth the risk.

After we leave the museum, we do the late lunch thing at this Irish-themed chain bistro place. I'm not prepared for leprechaun waiters—or at least little people who look an awful damn lot like them. I get a case of the giggles, but they don't seem to mind. The food's okay, but it's all mass-conjured so I'm not expecting much. While we eat, I can't help but think back to something my friend Natalie once mentioned about conjuration: anything made from thin air usually goes back to thin air after a few hours. Hmm. How does that work for food?

When our wait-leprechaun, Bix, returns to check on us, I ask if the food's going to disappear out of our system.

He laughs. "Aye, lass. You got a sharp mind on ya. But, rest assured. The entrees are real. They're not so much 'conjured' as prepared instantly. Now, the desserts... those are pure conjurations, so our guests can indulge without guilt."

"Oh, nice." Jason grins. "So that 2,000 calorie brownie and ice cream thing totally vanishes?"

Bix nods.

And on that note, when we're done with our entrée, we split that enormous brownie thing. Seriously, it's massive. If not for knowing it's a conjuration, I'd be ashamed of myself for ordering it as there's so much left when we're stuffed.

Eventually, we're both sitting in Jason's pickup truck feeling like whales and trying to figure out what to do with the rest of our day. Neither one of us much moves for a few minutes, too bloated to even speak.

"My place? Movies?" asks Jason.

I smile. "That works."

He grunts, pretending to be too fat to reach the gearshift.

"Ugh. Yeah. We probably could've skipped the brownie apocalypse."

"They only charged two bucks for it."

I rub my stomach. "That's because it's not real."

"Ugh. Yeah. Wish it would hurry up and get un-real."

Right around the time we arrive at Jason's house, I go from painfully full to content. His living room is even more 'bachelorized' than I remember it, and it's only been like a week since I've been here. Pizza boxes, Cheetos bags, and empty spring water bottles lay about at random.

Jason notices me noticing the mess and rushes around cleaning. Chuckling to myself, I pitch in. We fill a trash bag just from the living room, then proceed to flop on the couch and binge watch *The Emerald Order* on Netflix. It's a fictionalization of the Seven Kingdoms' War of 1914 that's trying to imagine what the 'Great War' would've been like had technology caught up to magic that long ago. I mean it's a little hard to believe machineguns or airplanes would've existed so long ago, but the scenes of dragons getting into midair fights with biplanes are kinda cool. It does, however, have *way* more sex than it needs... and so many character deaths. Sometimes, I think the writers are just trying to see how shocking they can make it. I half expect them to have the Red Baron sleep with his dragon. I mean everyone's already boinking their parents or siblings... they'd have to invoke draco-bestiality to be shocking at this point.

Anyway... four episodes in, a loud *boom* goes off somewhere in the distance.

"Whoa." Jason sits up.

I pause the TV. "Was that in the show or did that really happen?"

"Honestly? I can't tell."

We look around, listening, for a few minutes. When nothing else unusual occurs, we resume watching. About twenty minutes later, both our cell phones go off at once. Shit. It's *the tone.* I pull my phone out and, sure enough, find the automated notification from the station summoning all personnel.

"At least I don't need to take the bus." I stand and stuff the phone back into my pocket.

"Yeah. If we heard whatever that was explode, it's not going to be a pretty scene."

I cringe. "C'mon. Let's go."

HERLIHY FILLS THE DRIVER'S SEAT OF OUR RIG, AND HE'S TOO DAMN BIG to see past.

So, I stare out the side window at the reflection of our flashing lights on passing buildings. I'm seated directly behind him all kitted up. The gear never bothered me before, but lately, it's annoying. Mostly, because I know I don't need any of it to survive going into a fire scene. Still, my snow-white ass is staying incognito. Most places big enough to be called 'city' instead of town have wards on them preventing the trespass of magical creatures. No one bats an eye at a cockatrice, gryphon, or faerie out in the country, but I have no idea how people would react to a Shaar'Nath. Or a half-one like me. Humans get kinda uptight about the whole demon thing.

I'm not a demon.

Really.

Okay, I *look* like a demon but that's because some long-ago humans ran into Shaar'Nath and, well, they tend to have short tempers as well as violent, impulsive natures. Consequently, the humans of the day thought of them as 'demons.' Given that my sorta-people had been at war for tens of thousands of years with another extraplanar race, the Elestari, the arrogant pricks decided to turn humans against them. See, Elestari are all beautiful with feathery wings and perfect complexions. Humans started calling them 'angels' even though the Elestari *hate* that word. Humans don't mean it as an insult, but for whatever reason, it infuriates them.

So yeah, this whole belief system started up around 'demons' and 'angels' and some supreme being that's the king of the angels and some supreme bad dude who's the king of the demons... and yeah. War. Battle for human souls, all that fun stuff.

Only, neither the Shaar'Nath nor the Elestari could give one rat's ass about human souls.

The entire universe as we know it (and by we, I mean me plus humans) came into being as a barrier made by the Elestari and Shaar'Nath working together. *Gasp.* I know right? That's like seeing cats chasing dogs. I suppose when you've been killing each other for time immemorial and there's only a handful of both sides left, it's time to rethink one's life choices. Extinction sucks. So, they made a new dimensional plane as a barrier between Aesinor (where the snobs live) and Imbreleth (where my—sorta—people are from). None of them *wanted* to put anything in it. Like, if you build a fence to keep gophers out of your garden, you don't set about breeding bees *inside* the fence. But... somehow, humans happened. Guess all that creation-type-energy just kept on going.

Now, humans aren't important in the grand scheme of things. At least, not to the warring factions among the Shaar'Nath and the Elestari. They're kind of like mold growing on the wall. And the warmongers want to tear that wall down to allow war to resume, which isn't going to end well for the mold. Demons don't hate humans, Angels don't love them—both sides want them out of the way.

... and that's where I come in.

I'm supposed to destroy the entire plane, killing all humans on Earth—and I guess any alien civilizations that might be out there in space somewhere on any of the billion or so planets that could exist.

So yeah, nothing big. Yay me.

That's pretty tragic, but not as tragic as a damn eighteen-alarm fire on a Sunday evening interrupting my Jason time.

No, I'm not bitter. Seriously. Okay, I'm a little miffed at the universe for picking this moment to have a fire, but I don't begrudge running out here to help.

Herlihy rounds a corner, but jams on the brakes while honking at some idiot who doesn't understand the significance of a giant friggin' red truck covered in flashing red lights with a wailing siren.

"Hang on," I shout. "I got it."

I stick my head out the side window and stare at some shithead in a BMW who's not moving out of our way. Okay, the light *is* red, but still dude... move to the side. Snarling, I float the car into the air and send it careening into the nearest alley—sideways. Guy's got about two inches of clearance on both bumpers between buildings. Heh. Have fun with *that* K turn.

"Little rough?" asks Jason.

"That's my gentle," I sit back down. "If I was rough, the car'd be upside down."

"Holy shit," mutter Herlihy and O'Keefe simultaneously.

Another two blocks later, we hang a right onto I95, and *it* comes into view up ahead.

'It' being a giant column of fire rising into the dark night sky.

"Damn," says Humberto. "That's bad..."

"Natural gas processing plant went up." Herlihy shakes his head. "They're calling in everything within twenty-five miles."

I gulp. "Anyone hurt?"

"No idea." Humberto pokes at the laptop. "Nothing here about casualties yet."

A sick feeling settles in the pit of my stomach over the next few minutes as we keep driving and the orange light grows more intense. Within a half mile of the site, it feels like we've left Earth behind and gone into an apocalyptic hellscape. *Everything* around us is orange and fire-colored. Soon, we roll past some fire crews on the left, the guys hosing down the faces of buildings in an apartment complex across the street from the gas plant. It takes me a few seconds to realize the first two rows of buildings are little more than scattered toothpicks on top of concrete slabs.

A deafening roar comes from the pillar of Hades, so loud I can barely even think. It's like an entire fleet of military jets sit on the ground with their engines at full blast.

Jason tries to yell something, but I can't hear him. He tries again, and my best guess is 'F this is loud.'

I nod.

Herlihy pulls the truck to the side, rolling onto gravel, then slows to a stop by a large crowd of other fire engines.

We disembark, grab air tanks and hats, and hurry around front—but stop where Lieutenant Sims corrals us all at a demarcation line. Barely a hundred yards ahead from that point, cars melt where they stand, body panels and tires glooping off them fast enough to see in real time. Holy shit, it looks like someone put toy plastic cars in an oven.

Sims is *almost* audible using an electric megaphone. He says something about too hot to approach, worried about explosion, and waiting for the gas company to cut the line. I barge past the group of firefighters, some of whom aren't from our station, and pat Sims on the shoulder.

He makes eye contact, so I try to see if I've gotten any better with telepathic communication. *Can you hear me?*

Sims taps the side of his head, then tilts his hand back and forth in a 'sorta' gesture. His surface thoughts give away that he can barely hear my telepathy over the roar. When I mouth 'what happened?' he thinks about an eighteen-inch wide natural gas pipeline rupturing, burning too hot for anyone to get near it. Then, he thinks, *shit, even you'd probably have a rough time with this.*

I grin. Challenge accepted. Okay, so shouting and mental communication aren't working. I pull out my phone and open a note window. ‹Anything I can do?›

He looks at it, takes my phone, and types back ‹There's supposed to be a valve. Command wants to wait for it to burn out, but the company people think the main holding tank could explode if the fire backfeeds the line. That's why were' hanging back.›

I nod and grab the phone. ‹If that thing explodes, we're not far enough away.›

Sims flashes a weak smile and thinks that it'll wipe out everything in about 2,000 feet. Probably destroy the oil refinery east of here and light that on fire as well.

I type, ‹Well, shit. That sounds bad. Gonna go talk to that valve.›

He grabs my arms and yells 'be careful.' I don't hear it at all, but it's easy to pick out of his thoughts.

Nodding, I pat him on the shoulder, type ‹Plz hold my phone›, and trot off away from the group of firefighters, heading for a big rectangular building of corrugated steel that should give me a fair amount of cover from wandering eyes. Once out of sight behind it, I ditch my hat, air tank, and heavy coat.

"Well, time to see if this works." I pat the small lump in my shirt where the amulet Natalie made for me—a little chibi succubus—sits against my skin. According to her, if I change forms while wearing clothes, it'll magically absorb them. Normally, a full shift (as I call it) shreds my shit. Gaining two feet of height, wings, tail, and armor plating tends to do bad things to my clothes.

Since time is of the essence, I risk not taking the time to strip manually first, and get my demon on. Okay, I do spare the two seconds it takes to look around and make sure no one is watching. A split second before I surge taller, I'm stark naked. My armor plated exoskeleton appears faster than the speed of *eep*. Again, not that I care so much about being nude outside. Did that plenty enough growing up. More so that it's no longer considered 'cute' as an adult… and I'm allergic to cops.

My eyes become pools of dark sapphire energy—which is awesome. Smoke doesn't bother them at all. In fact, in this form I can see much better in the middle of a fire than using my human eyes out of a fire.

The roar is so loud I don't hear my wings unfurl. Before anyone can come to check on why I ran around behind this place, I leap straight up, powering into the sky. My flight is more magical in nature than physical. The wings are mostly for steering or serving as parachutes. I go where I will myself to go. And, anywhere other than face first into the side of a high-rise is a win for me. We don't really talk about my first time trying to fly.

After putting about five hundred feet between me and the ground, I lean forward out of the vertical ascent and orient myself toward the column of burn. With my Shaar'Nath eyes, what had once been a blinding streak of orange has become mesmerizingly beautiful. Individual threads of fire flutter about like long hair underwater, outlining slight variances in pressure and temperature by gradations in hue and brightness. The outermost surface has a rich blue color due to plentiful oxygen, while the majority of the column is orange inside.

I head toward it, entering a dive about a hundred feet from the pillar of flames. This thing's as big around as an old tree and... feels warm. Oh wow. If it's warm to me, this shit is effing *hot*. I faintly remember from training that natural gas in air burns around 3,500 degrees. But, yeah, I don't have time to gawk. And damn is this loud. I feel like I've stuck my head into the engine of that rocket they used to go to the moon... at least for noise.

Mostly wanting to make the damn roaring stop, I hurry into a dive way faster than simple falling. About fifty feet up, I flare my wings out and flip myself around to put my feet down. I come in a little hot— pun intended—landing in a three point stance on one knee with a fist in the ground... and crack the concrete.

Okay, crashed a little hard, but it didn't hurt. I stand and look around, whistling at two small sheds nearby that have become puddles of aluminum. The burn starts about six feet above a jagged gash in a white-painted pipe, but the fire seems to be creeping down. Something tells me that if the flame goes inside the breach, it's going to get all the way back to a giant reservoir tank and kaboom. The exploding gas won't be half as deadly as the shrapnel from a tank that big. Half-inch steel moving at a few kajillion miles per hour is a bit much for a Band Aid.

Or a Lifemage.

Yeah, not even they can put someone back together from being reduced to a puddle of ketchup.

Blackening scorches the pipe below the hole, despite no flame being that close to the metal. Similar black lines trace over the gravel in a jagged path that suggests an electrical discharge. I also pick up on a weird feeling in the air that I can't quite explain. It's almost like I've gone into a cloud of caffeine and my armor plated skin prickles with energy. Even though I'm naked in a technical sense, my full shift form (all seven feet of it) feels more like I'm wearing lightweight armor somewhere between crab shell and futuristic soldier. It looks like a suit more than bare skin, too: no nipples or other exposed bits. The plating is both rigid and has feeling, which is a totally bizarre sensation.

Hmm. At a guess, I'd say lightning struck the pipe, but that's odd. This pipe isn't the tallest metal object in the area. That would be a platform about twenty yards to the right—with a lightning rod. Something isn't adding up here. Said platform also has a bunch of equipment on the side of the pipe along with a huge red valve wheel. Bingo. A quick hop-flight gets me there in seconds. I ain't got time for stairs. Alas, the valve wheel pulls apart in my hands like unbaked pizza dough. Shit. The steel melted. That's bad. Very bad.

This platform stands about 200 yards from a huge pressurized tank, the source of the presently burning gas. Hopefully, there's another valve closer down the line that hasn't melted. I leap up onto the pipe and sprint down the length, careful to avoid gouging new holes in it with my toenails. That'd siphon off pressure and let the flame creep inside and... I'll probably wind up in outer space.

I spot another valve station at the 100-yard point and jump down from the pipe to the grating platform. The entire steel deck shakes. My landing likely would've made a big *clank,* but the roar is so damn loud and pervasive, I didn't hear a damn thing. Silence is going to feel alien if I can get this thing to stop.

It's noticeably cooler here, so I'm hopeful that this valve hasn't also goo-i-fied. The steel ring doesn't bend under my grip, and it's fairly easy to spin closed. Then again, I am a smidge stronger than the average girl. As fast as I can swing my hand around, I power the thing closed, trying to race the pressure drop. The valve stops with a metal-on-metal *thud* that I kinda hear over the burn.

Seconds later, the pressure drop kills the flame column, but also lets the burn into the breach. From the left of the valve housing, the whole pipe shudders with a heavy *whud*. The concussion of what's basically a 100-yard long eighteen-inch diameter shotgun firing hits me like a stiff punch over my entire body.

Most of the segments swell, a few blow open entirely. A few dozen half-inch-thick screws take off like bullets as the seams separate, ricochets echoing from as far back as where all the fire trucks are parked.

Best of all, the damn roaring has stopped. Holy shit I can hear my thoughts again—and the random clanks and thumps of pipe bits falling back to the ground all around me.

Actually, amend that. Best of all, the big holding tank didn't explode.

It probably won't be too long before I'm no longer alone here. The area's still superheated, but with the giant column of burning natural gas gone, it'll cool off pretty quick. I scramble upright and throw myself into the air, once again climbing straight up. This time, I concentrate on that 'do not see me' mental thing that I *still* need to ask my dad to teach me. No idea if what I think I'm doing is having any effect.

I swoop down for a landing behind the building I used for cover, and shift back to normal. Once again, I experience a split second of feeling naked before my clothes reappear on me. Oh, that is absolutely awesome. Best thing Natalie ever did for me is make this amulet. I am going to treat her for dinner at least the next twenty times we go out.

Luck is with me. No one comes to peek around the corner while I'm getting my coat and air tank back on. Carrying my helmet, I jog around the corner and head back in among my fire crew.

Lieutenant Sims catches my eye and gives me a knowing wink.

I trot up to him. "Got my phone?"

"Yeah." He hands it to me.

‹Damn nice work› is on the screen.

# 3

# ANGELS

Monday.

Actual Monday, which is still my day off. Two showers last night *almost* got the stink of natural gas out of my hair. Out of sheer laziness, I didn't bother getting dressed after the shower or upon waking up this morning. Irritatingly enough, mundane clothing doesn't really do much for keeping me warm. I could go outside in the winter in a bikini or a parka and it would feel about the same. Also, I'm lazy. Even as a kid, I found clothing annoying, much to Mom's frustration. Guess it's an innate thing.

Now that I think about it, I'm guessing fabric doesn't last too long in Imbreleth. The place literally has fire everywhere according to Dad. Well, flames and lots of black rock. Oh, and lava. Great place to work on a tan if you're looking for a dark shade of charcoal. Let's just say it's not exactly ranked on the top ten vacation spots for humans. Actually, I'm overstating it. Humans *can* survive there if they're careful.

That, of course, gets me wondering if Shaar'Nath walk around naked all the time 'back home.' Well, there's the armor at least. That at least covers the naughty parts. It's pretty clear that neither my kind, nor the Elestari even have any concept of embarrassment—at least over lack of attire. I wonder how humans wound up being so uptight about it. Okay, to be fair, not *all* humans are like that. A few tribal societies still exist here and there.

And wow, it sounds strange to talk about humans like I'm not one.

Draped on my sofa, I munch on a breakfast burrito while not quite watching TV. Fortunately, my evil rune oven decided not to mess with it. I'm too distracted thinking about the fire scene from yesterday to pay much attention to what's on the screen, only vaguely aware of shifting colors and a guy murmuring about enchanted anti-aging skin cream.

The brass decided to call it a lightning strike, officially categorizing the fire as an accident. Their theory is that something hit the pipe and tore a hole. Natural gas leaked out without flame for long enough to roll across the street into the apartment complex. Fortunately, the *bang* of the initial rupture scared the shit out of everyone over there, so they all ran outside before ignition happened. A wave of fire flew across the street and the first couple of apartment buildings, which had been filled with gas, exploded like bombs.

The fire's casualty count amounted to a handful of tropical fish, two hamsters, and an elderly woman who had a heart attack when the apartment building next door to her turned into toothpicks. Mostly she died because no one could hear her wheezing for help over the roar.

Speaking of… I can *still* hear that damn noise.

If this had happened on a weekday, the gas company probably would've lost about thirty guys. The yard only had a security guard on duty, and he'd been inside a building far enough away not to suffer serious injury.

So damn lucky.

Almost *too* lucky, like someone intentionally targeted a time for minimal casualties. And that weird energy in the air. I haven't been able to figure out what it means, though I'm tempted to say magic. That's pretty par for the course for the world. Don't understand something? Must be magic.

Only, most of the time, it turns out to be correct.

Flickering orange draws my attention to the television, where the news shows a field of big metal tanks burning. The reporter announces that authorities are blaming a lightning strike for the blaze, but the caption at the bottom of the screen reads 'suspicious fire at NJ oil refinery.' Huh. That's odd. I mean, it's not *that* far away. The same storm might have been responsible for both fires, but usually, storms don't leave an arcane charge in the air. I suspect magic is involved somehow, but bleh. Someone else can worry about that.

I'm feeling particularly lazy today.

---

VIDEO GAME NOISES DRAG ME AWAKE.

Ashley's flopped on the couch beside me in a denim skirt and pink top, no shoes, staring at the screen. The PlayStation is on and she's merrily guiding a cute little fox-man around a maze of huge carrots and vegetables. She's likely been there for a while and didn't bother waking me up, nor does she seem to care that I'm not dressed. Okay, more than a little awkward. Maybe I should rethink my policy of just letting her walk in whenever she wants. Well, okay, I *did* tell her she's not to come in if I'm not home.

"Hey," says Ashley, blasé as anything. "Your phone's exploding and you didn't wake up."

"Little tired." I rub my eyes and yawn. "Who was it?"

She shrugs. "I dunno. The phone's in your bedroom."

"Right."

I get up and trudge down the hall, grabbing the first long T-shirt I stumble across from the floor and pulling it on. On my way out of my bedroom, I telekinetically yank the phone off my nightstand into my hand. Natalie's called me like twenty times in a row, spaced five minutes apart to the second. Wow. I hope she's using an app to do that.

Redial.

"There you are!" shouts Natalie by way of greeting. "What happened?"

"Nothing. Just tired. Ash said you're exploding the phone. Something wrong?"

She laughs. "No. Just wondered if we were still on tonight?"

"Oh." I biff myself in the forehead. "Duh. Yeah. 'Mon over whenever."

"Cool. See ya soon."

The high-energy grin projected by Natalie's voice makes me smile. I pull some hair around in front of my face and sniff it. Blargh. Still reeks of natural gas and 'burning stuff.' Grumbling, I head back to the living room.

"Hey. Nat's coming to pick us up. Gonna go out for food."

"Cool!" chirps Ashley. "I like food that won't try to eat me."

"Ha. Ha. So... I still smell like a fire scene. Gonna grab a shower, 'kay?"

She nods.

A hot shower plus an inordinate amount of shampoo manages to reduce the stink in my hair to the point where no one will notice it unless they jam their face directly into my mane. Maybe I ought to get a hair wand one of these days. As much of a stigma as I've given them, cleaning, styling, and drying my hair in a few seconds would be worth the $800 price tag. Back in high school, a handful of the popular girls had them, so I developed this association between pricey beauty products and uptight, snobby bitches. That and $800 hurts. Then again, those things pretty much last forever unless broken, so it's like buying a lifetime supply of shampoo and conditioner. Well, maybe not for me. My 'lifetime' is considerably longer than a human's, so I'd probably need a new one every sixty years or so. Meh. Maybe I will get one if I can ever budget that much money out at once.

So, I do it the usual way—with a towel.

Once dry, I throw on this gothic black babydoll top with lacy cuffs over jeans and spend a while on eye shadow. Today feels like a black lipstick day... and I add these cute broadsword earrings that almost touch my shoulders. Grinning at myself in the mirror, I let my horns out. I probably could leave them visible and anyone looking at me would think they're attached to a headband or something. Nah. The horns are a bit extra for a steakhouse.

My horns vanish in wisps of smoke as I stand and return to the living room. Ashley's still in one piece, staring intently at the game. The doorbell announces Natalie's arrival before I can sit down again. Ashley pauses the game and follows me to the door.

"Where are your shoes?" I ask.

"Home." She shrugs. "You didn't tell me we were going out."

"Okay. Grab 'em then."

She nods.

I open the door to reveal my friend Natalie, who's gone totally normal. Sweatshirt and jeans with sneakers. Hmm. Maybe I over-gothed it tonight? Nah. No such thing.

Natalie jumps into a hug, then waves at the kid. "Hey! Ooh, cute earrings."

"Hey." Ashley returns the wave and darts out into the hallway, pulling two keys on a string out from under her shirt.

"Thanks."

Natalie reaches over and cradles one of my earrings. "You just gave me an idea."

I raise an eyebrow.

"Enchanted versions that grow into real swords when activated."

"Hmm. Wouldn't that be concealed carry?"

She shrugs. "Uhh... *sword* of."

I raspberry her.

"Seriously, though. I don't think that applies to blades."

"Might want to check on that first."

"Why? I'm not going to be wearing them, just selling them." She fakes an innocent smile. "I don't need the permit to conceal weapons as a dealer, and I already have the license to sell volatile enchants as long as I do the Federal Arcane Controlled Enchantments background check."

Ashley emerges from the next-door apartment having added flip flops. Guess my lazy mood's rubbed off on her. Bleh. Good enough.

We head downstairs and outside. Natalie goes right to the curb and fiddles with a ring.

"Where's your car?"

"He's coming." She grins.

A moment later, her little cream-colored Scarab rounds the corner and rolls up to us. I swear the thing's been enchanted to appear cute. The headlights have eyelashes that blink, and a slight curve to the front grille makes it appear to be smiling. Though the car is a super compact, the seats have enchants that make them feel like high-end recliners.

I *could* get a magic car that drives itself. One doesn't need a driver's license for those—only a shitload of money. Normal car plus license is about a third the cost. Advantages of mass production vs. individual enchanters making one car at a time. Problem being, the magic cars *can't* break the speed limit. If I ever need to rush to the station house for a fire response, I'd be stuck driving like a grandmother.

We hop in, and Natalie—rather her car—drives us to The Dragonflame Grill. It's a chain steakhouse that's all over the country, and I highly doubt any actual dragons are involved. I remember reading somewhere they do all the cooking at one central location and portal them out to each location to save costs, which keeps the prices low. Oh, yeah, and they don't do the 'sit on a saddle and make a fool of yourself' thing on birthdays. No, this place has a fake dragon people sit on that flies them around the whole room. So it's 'make a fool of yourself and possibly break your neck.'

The Scarab drops us off by the door and heads into the parking lot to find a space for itself.

Alas, the place is mobbed. It's not quite bad enough that we decide to bail and go somewhere else. A teen in a green 'Dragonflame Grill' polo shirt and a floppy dragon baseball cap hands me a fake plastic dragon scale pager when I put in my name on the Scroll of Waiting, then quotes me a forty-minute wait.

Good thing we didn't really have plans for after.

Ashley oohs and ahhs at the medieval-themed décor, staring awestruck at the various illusions of dragon-related things all over the walls. None of the seats in the waiting area are open, so we stand there trying not to block the front doors. No matter where we go, we seem to always be in someone's way.

We stand there as best we can minding our own business for about ten minutes.

"Hey, mama," says a man from behind.

Natalie gasps.

A loud *bang* similar to a balloon popping makes me flinch, and a weird ozone-like smell overpowers the peanut-and-cologne ambiance of the waiting area. I whirl to my left and blink at a cowboy hat, flannel shirt, jeans, socks, and boots collapsing in a pile behind her. Ashley looks down at the clothes and giggles.

"What the heck just happened?" I ask.

Red-faced, Natalie scowls. "Some creep just grabbed my rear end."

"Since when do you have an ass of annihilation?" I raise an eyebrow.

Ashley bursts into laughter.

"No. It's a defensive enchantment on this belt." Grinning, Natalie pats the buckle. "It teleported him randomly off somewhere up to a mile." She bites her lip. "Well, not completely random. It won't throw someone straight up."

"Nice." I point at the floor. "And left his clothes behind."

A devilish grin parts her lips. "Yeah, that's on purpose. Both for revenge and because it actually makes the process a lot simpler. Apportation is a pain in the ass. You have to explicitly target every individual item, like socks count as two targets. The enchantment is much cheaper and easier only taking the living body."

"So portals are complicated?"

"No. Portals are portals. That opens a doorway. Apportation is point, click, poof."

"Oh. So the dude who grabbed your ass is now somewhere outside up to a mile away, bare ass naked?"

Natalie nods. "He shouldn't have grabbed me."

The kid's laughter proves contagious. I, too, burst into cackles.

No one else in the waiting area appears to have realized what happened. Just as well. Eventually, the plastic dragon scale in my hand goes nuts, flashing, vibrating, and emitting a 'magical' sound effect. We force our way through the crowd to the front desk. A tall, skinny guy with neat dreads, a huge grin, and dark brown skin takes the scale from me while introducing himself as Jared. He's young, probably still in college, and chats about how excited he is that we decided to visit him here while he shows us to a table and leaves a basket of little dragon-shaped breads. They're so cute I feel bad eating them, but the cinnamon-laced whipped butter is irresistible. Sorry little guys. You're delicious.

I think the Earth would legit stop rotating if an eight-year-old went to a restaurant like this and *didn't* order chicken fingers. True to form, Ashley requests that plus fries. While I'm not usually too keen on steak, since we're at a *steak*house, I break pattern and get one. Natalie must've been a wolf or something in a prior life—the girl's *all about* beef. Yeah, coming here tonight was her pick.

While waiting for our food, we start trying to guess where the idiot landed and what kind of awkward situation developed out there. That conversation leads into enchanting and I ramble a bit about my feelings on the hair wand. Mistake. Natalie thought I had one and now wants to make me one for free. I insist on at least paying for the materials, about $120. Ashley starts to open her mouth—likely to ask about a hair wand, too—but at hearing the price, she closes it. Nat gives me the 'I'm gonna give her one too and don't say a word' look.

A pair of cat-sized dragons fly over to our table carrying a tray. Jared follows close behind, taking each plate and setting it in front of us. After we assure him that everything's fine, he smiles and walks off, leaving us to our food.

We eat in relative quiet for a while until this smoking hot twenty-something blonde woman comes out of nowhere and slides into the bench seat with Natalie, who stares at her in bewildered surprise. She's wearing this white thing that can't decide if it's a shift dress or a toga.

Ashley, on my right, waves hello.

It takes me a second to realize the woman has red irises, at which point I recognize her face—Laniah, the Elestari who's so far proven *not* to be too much of an asshole. Actually, she saved Lawrence's life after that mage blew up the house... so maybe I should think of her in friendlier terms.

Grr. Another reason to dislike the stuck up 'angels.' I bet more than most can use life magic, but they rarely bother helping humans out.

Laniah leans her arms on the table, slouched as if exhausted, in pain, or both. "Hi. Sorry for just appearing like that, but I had to warn you."

Natalie glances at her, then me, then her. "She another, umm..."

"She plays for the other team," I say. "Though, I'm starting to become confused about the teams."

"You're an angel?" whispers Natalie.

Laniah's smile turns pained. "I've been called worse. Recently, in fact."

"Nat, They consider that an insult. Laniah's the only one I've run into so far that I care enough to make an effort not to use the word."

"Oh. Oops." Natalie offers a sheepish smile. "Sorry. Didn't know."

"It's okay. I didn't grimace because you said 'angel.' It doesn't bother me that much if someone's not using it on purpose as an insult." Laniah rubs her side. "Had a spirited disagreement not long ago."

"So... you said something about a warning?" I ask.

Ashley dumps more pepper on her fries.

"Yes." Laniah reaches over the table and grabs my hand. "There is a group of Elestari who are planning to attack you so you don't destroy the Armistice."

Oh for fuck's sake. I almost pound my fist into the table out of sheer anger, but manage to stop myself before our dinner goes flying across the restaurant. "Dammit! What's wrong with them? I have no intention of doing anything like that."

A few nearby people glance over at me for shouting, but since I didn't say anything too weird, they don't stare too long.

"I know… I know…" Laniah sighs. "We're not exactly talking about rational individuals."

"Is this like imminently critical?" I stop squeezing my fist closed before destroying the fork. "If you say too much more, I'm going to make a scene."

She shakes her head. "I think it can wait a couple minutes for you guys to finish."

Jared shows up to check on us, spots Laniah, and goes full on lovesick, staring at her. "Oh, hi. Can I get you anything?"

Laniah eyes our plates, all about half done, emits an apologetic sigh, and orders a salad.

"Got it. I'll put a rush on that so your friends don't have to wait." He nods, smiles at everyone, and hurries off.

Ashley waits all of ten seconds before blurting, "I thought angels are supposed to be good."

"One is," I mutter.

"Most of my kind believe they are, but they're too proud of themselves." She winks at Ashley.

"Why do they want to go back to war? That's bad." The kid picks up another piece of chicken.

I stare at the ceiling. "That's the million-dollar question. It's not like either side has defense contractors who stand to make money on killing. What started the war in the first place?"

Laniah shrugs. "No idea. I'm not *that* old. And most of us don't want war. The majority prefer not to live in constant fear of invasions."

"What's it like there?" I ask.

"Oh, you'd probably find it boring. Lots of meadows, trees, rolling grasslands. Crystal cities gleaming in the daylight."

"Do you have like day jobs and stuff?" asks Natalie around a mouthful of mashed potatoes.

Laniah laughs. "No… mostly we sit around and talk, or entertain ourselves by making art or going flying."

"Maybe they want to fight because they're just bored," says Ashley.

"It's a nice kind of boring there." Laniah smiles. "But, humans aren't... what's the term? 'Wired' for that? I think Aesinor is *too* peaceful for them to tolerate for long."

Natalie wags a fork at her. "I accept that challenge."

"If any human could tolerate a world like that, it'd be Nat." I wink at her.

We make minor chitchat for the rest of our meal, though an air of hurry hangs over us. Laniah picks up the whole tab on a credit card. Hey, cool. Whatever.

"You really didn't have to do that," says Natalie. "Now I feel guilty."

"Don't." Laniah smiles. "It's magic. We don't have banks."

I snicker at the thought of an 'angel' stealing. "Wait, you hit them with a bogus card?"

"Not really. Everyone thinks they get paid, but no one would ever be able to figure out where it came from."

"How?" Natalie gawks at her. "Payment machines have anti-theft enchantments."

Laniah quirks an eyebrow. "Humans are only starting to understand magic. To most of my people, humans casting spells is like training pet hamsters to play video games."

Natalie slouches. "Oh. Right."

"Burn," mutters Ashley. "And can I have a nicer cage?"

We all chuckle.

"Thank you for the food." Ashley looks at me and Laniah, not quite sure who to direct her comment to.

Laniah smiles at her while I pat her on the head.

Once Jared returns with the receipt, we make our way outside past the still-full waiting area. I head for a spot on the sidewalk out front far enough from the doors that a random blurted oddity won't cause problems.

"Okay... so what's going on?" I ask.

"The reason I'm a little sore is due to having to fight my way past some idiots. I'm really not the best spy." She rolls her right shoulder, cringing. "The other side, the fools who want war, are plotting to abduct your mother."

"What?" I shout, clenching my hands into fists. "Why?"

Laniah's expression is simultaneously consoling and radiating a 'yeah, I know, stupid' vibe. "They hope to force you to destroy the Armistice."

"Ooh!" I fume and start pacing. It's tempting to let my tail out purely so I can swish it back and forth in anger. "That's the dumbest thing I've ever fu—" I bite my lip, glancing at Ashley. "Ever freakin' heard. If I do what they want and destroy the Armistice, that means the entire world goes away—and my mother *still* dies. Everyone I care about dies. There's literally no way in hell threatening to hurt someone could possibly convince me to do that. Like, do these dumbasses think saying 'Kill your mom, or we'll kill your mom' is going to work?"

"Yeah, basically." Laniah folds her arms. "I mean, they *are* that dumb."

"Wow." Natalie blinks. "That is seriously stupid. Hey, can I ask an off-topic question?"

I stare at her with tears in my eyes.

"Never mind. It can wait." Natalie puts a hand on my arm. "You okay?"

Ashley leans back. "The last time she made that face, she threw a bad guy out a window."

A thought crosses my mind that I dare not even give voice to. Maybe they think if they destroy everything I love, I'll come down with a bad case of the fuckits and stop caring about ending the world.

"No. I'm having a not-okay moment." A lump swells in my throat. Gah. I haven't felt like crying this bad since my first time spending the night in a holding cell at eleven. "If they hurt Mom, I swear... I'll do the only thing I can to give them a giant middle finger. I'll end myself. Then they *can't* destroy the Armistice."

"No!" shouts Ashley, leaping into a hug. "Don't!"

Ugh. This isn't my kid. Why am I about to blow up and cry all over her?

"Brook, no fuckin' way." Natalie's grip on my arm tightens. "You're not gonna do anything like that."

"If it's the only way to stop those shitheads from hurting you guys?"

Laniah brushes a hand over my cheek. "Don't give in to despair. Those plotting to reignite the war are a small group." She lets her arm fall to her side. "I'll keep an eye on your mother until they abandon this foolish idea. They will eventually realize how idiotic it would be for them to use the threat of harm against humans to coerce you into killing all humans."

"Wow... really?"

She nods.

"Thank you." I stare at her with new respect and—dare I say it— love. Not like I wanna jump her, more like she's become a dear friend even though I've only known her for a couple weeks and don't really even *know* her. It pisses me off feeling this vulnerable and needing help from someone, but I'm not going to be a dumbass and turn my nose up at her out of pride.

"I thought they didn't really hate us?" asks Natalie.

"They don't." I wipe my cheeks, trying to act like I didn't just go all emo. "It's our dimension they hate because it stops them from bashing the shit out of each other."

Laniah glances out over the parking lot. "It is taking some effort to convince allies that you share our mindset, but we are making some progress. Don't lose hope yet. Okay?"

I nod. "Yeah. Not sure why I went down Sad Street. Usually, I take the shortcut to Fury Ave."

"What did you want to ask?" Laniah glances at Natalie.

"Oh, umm." Nat keeps her arm around me. "Just being a magic nerd. It's not important."

"Go ahead." I laugh. "I'm good."

She grins. "Well, I was just wondering if you can use magic to heal like a Lifemage, why are you still sore and stuff?"

"Injuries inflicted to our kind by certain weapons in the Armistice cannot be healed with magic." Laniah nods toward me. "Her claws and Elestari blades are magical in nature. When Elestari or Shaar'Nath cross into this plane, our energy is in a state of imbalance."

"That's why if you die, you just go home?" I ask.

"Correct. Though, such a journey leaves us weakened for some time and unable to cross the boundary until we've recovered."

"What happens if someone hurts Brook?" Ashley squeezes me.

"More than likely, she would lose her anchor to the Armistice and be catapulted into Imbreleth. She would cease being part human, as that part will have died. Over the next century or so, she would gather energy from the plane of her origin until she becomes a Shaar'Nath—or the process may fail and she would cease to be."

I blink. "Well, that sounds lovely. Definitely not on my list of shit to do. How messed up is it that the pacifists want to kill me?"

Laniah brushes her hair off her face, tucking it behind her ear. "They don't see it as killing you as much as sending you home. Only in your present form are you able to enter the Pillars of Creation and destroy them. If you survived your human 'death,' you would be a Shaar'Nath and unable to enter."

"Yeah. I remember. Pure bloods can't go in there... nor can humans. Pretty good security making it such a pain in the ass to do."

"Hey, ladies."

We all turn at a group of three men in flannel shirts walking up to us on their way into the restaurant... probably heading for the bar.

"Like three angels," says the guy on the left, smiling.

Much to my surprise, their intentions aren't scummy.

"She might be an angel"—I nod toward Laniah—"but I'm a little more of a devil."

Ashley starts snickering.

"You girls waiting for someone?" The dude on the right edges closer to me.

"Nah, we're actually done eating already. Girls' night out and all," I say in a polite tone since they're not giving me creep vibes.

"Cool." Middle guy nods. "Okay. Take it easy."

"You too," I say.

Natalie nods. Laniah waves.

The three head off into the restaurant.

"So bad." Natalie play-punches me in the arm.

"What?"

"Angels and devils?" She rolls her eyes. "They had no idea you were being kinda literal."

"Yeah…"

"I should be going." Laniah attempts a reassuring smile. "Don't lose too much sleep."

"Thanks for keeping an eye on Mom."

"You didn't ask to be put in this position. It's the least I can do." She flashes this little patronizing smile, but I don't let it get to me.

In a blink, she's gone. None of the people waiting outside react at all.

"Whoa. Neat trick." Natalie blinks. "Self-teleportation with simultaneous cognition deflection."

Ashley stares up at her like she'd spoken some alien language.

"So, what now?" asks Natalie.

"Well…" I glance at the sky, beyond tempted to fly straight to my mom's place and check on her. "Gimme a sec?"

Natalie nods.

I take a few steps off and call Mom. She's home, fine, and thinks I'm being paranoid, acting as though I never even showed her my wings. As soon as I mention heading up there to check on her, she insists she's about to go to sleep. We go back and forth for a bit until she accepts that I'll visit her tomorrow. Sigh. Great. Sleepless night time. Still, with Laniah keeping an eye on her and me having Ashley to watch…

I say goodnight with Mom, hang up, and walk back over to Natalie and Ashley. "Probably movies or PlayStation at my place."

"Sorry," mutters Ashley.

I laugh, and ruffle her hair again. "Don't be. Those are the usual two choices. Our social life isn't exactly wild anymore."

"A warm, cozy couch and comfortable PJs *is* a great time. And yes, I know we're tragically uncool." Natalie holds the back of her hand to her forehead like some old-timey actress in a drama. "So tragically uncool."

Ashley laughs.

Her Scarab rolls up to the curb beside us.

"Time to go. Our limo's arrived." I pull the door open for the kid like a chauffeur.

"Wow." Ashley settles in the back. "These seats are so small only a kid *could* ride back here."

"She may be small..." Natalie pats the dashboard. "But I love her."

The car vibrates as if in response.

Wow. I'll never get used to that.

# 4

## A LITTLE ROUGH

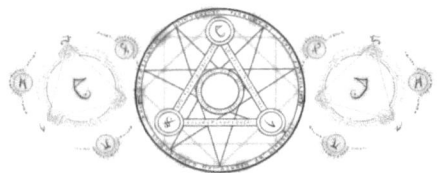

Tuesday is remarkably mundane.

It's my Monday, so I have to go into the station. Worrying about Mom kept me from really sleeping well, so the quiet day is beyond welcome. When my shift ends, it's time for cheating. And by cheating, I mean skipping the damn bus. Taking a PEPTA portal to Allentown—where Mom lives—costs about twelve bucks and takes mere seconds. However, waiting for them to open the portal could be up to an hour.

So, I head out the back of the station where everyone goes to vape, spend a moment concentrating on my 'no one see me' mental projection, and pull off my department polo shirt. Of course, I'd planned this as soon as I woke up today so I've got a racerback top on under it.

Tendrils of black smoke exude from my back, spreading out roughly seven feet to either side before solidifying into my wings. I hurl myself straight up and climb up a couple thousand feet to stay away from prying eyes.

Since I'm still kinda shitty at navigation, I check my phone to point myself toward Allentown, and fly. It doesn't take long before I have to shift my eyes to protect from windblast. Clouds of blue energy aren't as tender as physical eyeballs. Oh, neat: the GPS app tells me I'm doing about 340 miles an hour. It's kinda scary to think about Dad telling me the Elestari are better at flying. Does that mean just speed, or are they like more agile? Meh. Who cares?

About seven minutes later, I'm over Allentown.

Yeah, I'd still be waiting for the mage to open the portal. Actually, no. I'd probably still be on the bus not even at the PEPTA station yet. I slow down while flying in circles, searching for Mom's place. Allentown isn't too far from where I spent my childhood. I do kinda miss Quakertown, even if there wasn't much to do there other than stupid crap that got me picked up by the cops.

Eventually, I spot Mom's house and swoop in to land in the back yard. Grass is a bit long, but it's nearly fall so maybe she's going to let it coast. The instant I want them to, my wings dissolve to smoke and absorb into my back. I pull the polo back on, fluff my hair out the neck, and let myself in the back door with the keys Mom gave me.

"Mom? You here?"

"Ay! You scared me," yells Mom in Spanish from the hallway. She's probably in the living room. "What are you doing coming in the kitchen?"

I walk to the front of the house. Her living room's decorated in a mixture of pea-soup-green and grandmother. Wow. She's even doing the doily thing. It's anyone's guess if she's feeling prematurely old or this is some kind of subtle hint that she wants grandkids. The aroma of lemon furniture polish is nearly eye-watering.

Mom peers up at me from the sofa, still clutching her heart.

"Better to land in the yard. Decided to fly in since it's so much faster."

She gives me a strange look, almost like she's convinced herself she imagined me having wings. "So what's on your mind that you almost came up here in the middle of the night?"

"Mom..." I say in the same put-upon teenage voice I used to use, and flop on the couch. "A little after ten isn't the 'middle of the night.'"

"It is when you're my age."

"You're not old." I smirk. "You get up too early. Why do you still wake up at five? You work from home now."

She grins. "Old habits, and you know I am a morning person."

A 'morning person' I am not. The only thing standing between me and homicide before 11 a.m. on a typical day is a giant cup of coffee. That and laziness. Murder takes too much energy before noon— unless someone's about to hurt a person I care about. How messed up is it that literal killing is now a 'thing that's possible' for me? I sincerely doubt another Frank situation is going to occur next door, so I'm safe. When I talk about killing someone for daring to talk to me before coffee, I'm being cute.

Honest.

"Yeah. I remember." She used to drive me nuts in the morning as a kid. I mean, they already started school stupid early, and when she'd been wide awake for over an hour before I had to get out of bed... ugh. There's nothing more annoying to a not-morning person than someone who's too cheerful too early. "But seriously, this is important."

Mom sets down her notepad. Must be in the process of planning a new book. *Why* she jots down notes with a physical pen and paper, I can't even guess. So much easier to type on a computer. "I thought you gave up smoking that stuff."

"I did. Remember what I told you a couple weeks ago about the Armistice and the two sides? I just found out that the ones who want war might try to threaten or kidnap you to make me do what they want."

She gives me the same disbelieving expression she hit me with every time I tried to lie my way out of trouble as a kid. "You didn't get into any of that funny weed again, did you?"

"No. I haven't touched that shit since I was seventeen."

Mom looks down at the notebook in her lap for a silent moment. "I'm sorry, Brooklyn."

"For what?" I raise an eyebrow.

"Not being around as much as I should have been."

I sit up, scoot closer, and put an arm around her. "Mom, you were a single mother busting your ass to support a kid. You've got nothing to apologize for." My turn to stare down. "I should be the one apologizing to you. Sorry if I was a little rough on you growing up."

Mom chuckles. "A little?"

That gets a cheesy smile from me. "Yeah. Cut me some slack, huh? My impulse control issues aren't entirely my fault."

She shakes her head. "You were certainly a handful."

"It all seemed fun at the time. Like when I rode that skateboard down the highway? I didn't really understand how bad that scared you."

Mom shudders. "My ghost almost leapt right out of me when the police told me what you did."

"Oncoming traffic," I say, wagging my eyebrows.

"Don't remind me."

"Hey you remember when the cops busted Fuckler?"

Mom gasps at me. "What?"

"Oops." I laugh. "Mr. Kunkler. He lived six trailers over from us. My friends and I all called him that because he was such a nasty son of a bitch."

"Yes, I remember him." Mom scowls. "That man didn't much like anyone or anything."

Charitable as always... I swear the woman can't say a mean thing about anyone. "So the cops got him for growing weed."

She laughs. "He had to be selling it all. No one could be that uptight if they used that stuff."

I blink. My mother just made a pot joke. "Are you really my mother or did the Elestari replace you with a clone?"

"Brook." She frowns. "I know I used to give you a hard time over the drugs, but I was worried about you. I may be your mother, but even parents have senses of humor."

"I saw him grab you."

Mom glances sideways at me.

Carlos' Frisbee landed too close to the old bastard's trailer. We'd all been mostly nine or ten at the time, and Fuckler comes storming out the door and grabs Carlos by the arm, hauls him off his feet yelling at him in half-German half-English. So, being the fearless little hellion I was, I jumped right on his back and started pounding away. Carlos ran off, the old guy threw me to the ground and started screaming at me. Mom came running and got between us.

"I didn't run that far. I saw him grab you like he was going to hit you, but you looked him dead in the eye and told him to go ahead and do it, see what happens."

Mom squeezes my hand, a sad smile on her face. "Yeah. Fool thought I was threatening him with my 'gang friends.' Obviously, since I speak Spanish, I'm up to my ears in gang thugs."

"Most rational people wouldn't understand you meant divine retribution."

She sighs.

That's not an argument I'm even going to start. According to Dad, people invented religion after they saw Shaar'Nath and Elestari. Mom's really into religion, but she's one of the rare ones who doesn't use it as an excuse to be hateful. She loves everyone. If me showing her my wings and horns didn't change her mind, nothing will. Heck with it if it makes her feel better.

"But yea, those weed plants? Me."

She blinks.

"Found some seeds in a bag I got and decided to plant them."

"He almost went to prison," says Mom in a raised voice. "How could you do something like that?"

"Mom, *no one* in that place liked him. He was mean and nasty to everyone. And, the cops did eventually believe him when he said someone else planted them."

"What would you have done if he'd gone to prison for twenty years?"

I raise both eyebrows. "Other than laugh my ass off?"

She sputters.

"I'm surprised you're upset at me for getting him arrested and not at my having a bag of weed at eleven."

"You think I didn't notice." Mom pats me on the knee. "I did what I could to raise you right, even if I didn't always have the time to spend with you... or the time to get into an argument. The bag did walk away, didn't it? Wasn't in the stuffed dragon when you went back for it."

I stare at my mother in stunned silence. For so long, I thought she'd remained oblivious to me getting high until after the fire and we'd moved. That night the cops told her they caught me under the influence, she'd known I'd been experimenting for years already. "I totally screamed at Vicky about that. I thought she stole it. That almost ended our friendship."

"I'm sorry. I should've told you I got rid of it, but..."

"It's okay. You were always so damn tired. No matter what I did, I was never upset with you. Even when I stole the car to get ice cream."

Mom fans herself. "You tried to give me three heart attacks a week."

"What? You were tired. I wanted ice cream." I chuckle. "Really, I appreciate everything you did. Might not have shown it back then, but I love you, Mom."

She leans against me. "You're in for a heck of a ride if your kids are anything like you."

"Might be a bit of a wait on that."

"That Jason you're with now seems nice, at least the way you speak about him."

I shrug one shoulder. "He is. And I dunno, maybe he'll be the one. But, I've only been dating him for... not even a month yet. Bit early to talk about kids. Plus, I have that small issue of destroying the world to worry about. If I spawn, the 'forces of evil' might try to use my kids to do what I'm refusing to do."

"That again?"

"Yes." I glance at her. "That again. It's not exactly shoplifting a PlayStation."

"I'm worried about you, Brook. These things you think you're seeing lately. Maybe I didn't want to believe the signs, but the way you were growing up, now this... maybe it's time we see a doctor."

Facepalm.

"Mom... I'm not schizophrenic." I stand, face her, and shift fully into Shaar'Nath form—in all my seven-foot tall armor plated, horned glory. My right wing accidentally swats a bunch of portraits off a tiny table with a doily.

I really love the amulet Natalie got me. Not having to manually strip to spare my clothing from destruction is awesome.

My mother gawks at me.

"If I'm hallucinating, you are too," I say, my voice noticeably deeper in this form. "I am still the same daughter you remember, only with a few extra features... and a buttload of new problems. No, I'm not a demon. I'm not evil. We went over all this before. Alternate dimensions, that sort of thing?"

"Yes. I... thought I might've dreamed it." She shivers, looking way too small and frightened to be my mother.

At least she doesn't appear frightened of *me*, more of her reality shattering.

I change back to normal and the amulet covers me once more in my clothes: white fire department polo, black BDU pants, and sneakers.

Mom stands into a hug. "Brooklyn, what's going on?"

"I've got it handled. It'll be fine. Not like this is the end of the world... oh wait."

She makes a noise somewhere between laugh and sob. "That's not at all funny."

"If anything weird shows up, tell them it's stupid for them to take you. They'd basically be saying 'kill your mother or we'll kill your mother.'"

Mom scrunches her eyebrows together. "You're right. That doesn't make any sense. Well, you are here. Come, I will make us something to eat."

"I'm twenty-three. You don't have to cook for me. I can help." I squeeze her hand. "Promise me you'll at least be careful."

"Of course," says Mom, still sounding like she's not taking the situation too seriously. "And I don't mind cooking for you. You're still my daughter. But, if you want to help, come on."

I follow her toward the kitchen, shaking my head. Honestly, now that I think about it, what good is it asking her to be careful? What could she possibly do to stop Shaar'Nath or Elestari coming after her?

Damn. Maybe Natalie could help me figure something out.

For now, I'll have to settle for being a guard-demon.

And making pastelis.

# 5

## FOLKLORE

The next day, my laziness manifests in the form of taking the bus to work like a normal person who doesn't own a car. It does take longer to get to the station, but I can't nap while flying. And being spotted on a bus won't upend my entire life the same way a poorly timed picture could.

Great. So much for napping.

As if I'm not already worried enough about Mom, my brain runs away with trying to guess how the world would react to my true nature. Would the government decide to classify me as a magical creature and kick me out of the city? Some of those cults are kinda particular about their mythology. Living proof that the world isn't what they want everyone to believe wouldn't go over well. I'm sure some will label me a demon and call for my head on a pole, and the ones who do accept the truth would still probably try to get rid of me to protect their little stories.

Or ugh. Another thought hits me that's even worse.

What if I'm not supposed to literally destroy any sort of pillar? What if the entire point of my existence *is* to be discovered, poke holes in the humans' mythology, and cause mass confusion, holy wars, and perhaps even Armageddon? My impulsive nature and tendency to play fast and loose with rules is exactly the recipe for being discovered eventually.

Wait. No. That can't be right. It doesn't make any sense that throwing human society into chaos would destroy the entire plane of existence. Humans are the ones who are arrogant enough to claim some great supreme being created all of known space, yet only seems to care about life on one tiny planet among tens of billions.

We're mold growing on the walls of a fish tank.

Well, *they* are. I guess I'm not really human after all. Anyway, that 'mold' doesn't only grow in one spot. It's a veritable certainty that out of all those planets, life has happened somewhere else, too. Okay. That's good at least. I don't have to worry about blowing up an entire dimension merely for getting caught with my wings out.

Besides, if it was that easy, the warmongers would've shown themselves to humans centuries ago. Kinda makes me wonder why they don't—at least in large numbers. One-off sightings happen, but you'd think they wouldn't feel the need to hide.

They ought to just find a nice open field somewhere... or better yet, go to the Moon and kill each other up there. Sorta like pan-dimensional paintball with better special effects. Though, that would basically be little more than violence-masturbation as none of them would die permanently. Those idiots want to exterminate the other species entirely. Which is super confusing since they're presently working together to find a way to force me to tear down the Armistice. How fucked up is that? They find common ground to help each other, but the end goal is genocide of the very people they're working alongside.

Hmm, maybe Humans aren't the dumbest critters in the universe.

The bus pulls over at my stop, interrupting my thoughts. Good. I need a break from that crap anyway. Worry about Mom occupies me for the two block walk to the station house along with the sense that I'm being watched. I squint up at the sky trying to catch a glimpse of an Elestari sneering down his nose at me, but the only interesting thing among the clouds is a smallish blue dragon.

Huh. That's kinda rare here. The US doesn't have much in the way of dragons, nor do I know enough about them to identify where it's from. Natalie once told me an experienced dragonologist can determine the country, even region, of origin based on the shape of the head, nose, horns, around the jaw and such. About the only dragons I can tell apart are the Chinese ones. They're way obviously different from the European ones.

My hopes for a quiet day shatter with an alarm call a little after noon. We scramble to the rig and head out to the scene of a small kitchen fire, basically a pan of grease and some blackening on the wall. No injuries and no significant amount of property damage, though the guy who failed at cooking is a little rattled.

While I'm standing there watching O'Keefe hose the pot down with a powder-based extinguisher, a small enchanted mirror at the corner of the counter catches my eye with a news broadcast about a lightning strike and fire at a chemical plant in North Jersey. A scene of flashing emergency lights and fire fills the 'screen' behind the reporter.

"… started late last night and is still burning. Fire crews are working to contain the blaze despite several resounding explosions from inside the building. Fragments of storage tanks have come down in residential areas over a mile away. Additional hydromancers are en route to offer support, even tapping several students in their senior year of Academy. Authorities expect to have the blaze contained within the hour. For ANN, I'm Miles Prescott."

The mirror turns black with an 'Arcane News Network' logo for a few seconds before the two studio anchors come back.

Hmm. Odd. Some normal people get enchanted mirrors instead of televisions since they're super thin and don't die when the power goes out, but they don't exactly work with DVD players or streaming services. And the news channels—well channel—they get is skewed toward magey stuff.

"Whoa," says O'Keefe. "Check that out."

I follow his pointing finger to a row of small jars lined up near the stove. Some of the contents appear to be moving. Worms, slugs, beetles, or some such. Ick.

"Guess he added the wrong seasoning to his lunch." I peer into the pan, which appears to contain a few pieces of chicken that he'd been attempting to fry.

O'Keefe chuckles.

Maybe the guy who lives here is a luminare, a partial mage like my mother. Other than the moving ingredients and a mirror, the row house looks normal. Mages tend to decorate in a certain way. But hey, I shouldn't generalize like that. Not everyone who can use magic runs around in a robe.

---

NOT QUITE TWENTY MINUTES AFTER WE MAKE IT BACK TO THE STATION, Lieutenant Sims pages me to his office.

Oh great. What did I do this time?

Grr. Probably nothing. I hate that my instinctual reaction whenever I'm summoned somewhere is to feel like I've been sent to the 'principal's office.' Admittedly, during school, it *did* mean I'd done something wrong. Lieutenant Sims looks up from his desk when I walk in, his short brown hair neat as always.

"What's up, LT?" I ask.

He gestures to his left. "Someone here to see you."

Lawrence Ellis, once again in his arson investigator uniform, turns away from Sims' shelf to smile at me. His afro's a little greyer than I remember, but he appears in good health.

"Holy shit!" I hurry over and hug him before the idea it might be inappropriate hits me. Meh. Don't care. "How are you doing with the recovery?"

"Heh." He pats me on the back a couple times and releases the hug. "And I'm all good. Back on duty."

"That's awesome! It's great to see you." I tilt my head. "Didn't you say you were going to retire?"

Lawrence chuckles. "I'm not quite there yet. Still only fifty-two. And yeah, had a close call, but it ain't like we're cops. Usually, my job's pretty safe pickin' through the aftermath. The Lifemage at the hospital was a little confused. Never saw anyone come back from a beating like that."

I bite my lip, thinking of Laniah using her magic while I flew him back to the city. Heh. She'd come up to yell at me for 'being obvious' and flying around, but... she saved his life. That crazy Lifemage who'd been making nazedeh while attempting to heal fatal injuries would shit his pants if he ever studied Lawrence's case. I can't help but remember her comment about humans only starting to learn magic when we asked her about that funny credit card. The idea of 'angels' stealing is kinda funny, but only due to the way mythology has framed them to the human experience. Most Elestari regard humans as ants, and I bet they also think money is a fairly silly concept as well.

"Yeah I bet that confused them." I give Sims the side eye, certain he has no interest in any talk about extraplanar matters.

"It's good to be back." He hooks his thumbs in his pockets and sighs. "And it figures I wind up on another weird one. Guess I've become the 'arcane specialist.' Anyway, that's why I'm here."

"Ahh. Sure. No problem. What's up?" I glance at Sims, fidgety. I half want to protest being thrown on an investigative assignment while I'm still on edge about my mother, but maybe having something else to focus on will help me deal. Sitting around staring at the walls and worrying would only make it worse.

"Not entirely sure yet," says Lawrence. "Got a small fire scene that appears to be of paranormal origin. At the moment, I was just hoping you could give it a psychic sniff."

"Assuming Sims is okay with it, sure."

The lieutenant nods. "Fine with me."

I follow Lawrence outside to a department SUV with Arson Investigator markings. Once we're both inside and underway, I look over at him expectantly.

"One of the oddest things I've ever seen in my career."

"Oh?" I ask.

He leans back in the seat, left hand grasping the wheel, right arm draped in his lap. "Weirdest goddamn thing. Though I s'pose not as weird as having a statue come to life and try to kill you."

"That's good. First golem for me, too."

"All that what happened… that really happened?"

"Yeah."

"You're…"

"A little extra." I flash an innocent smile. "I know what I look like, but don't believe what you hear. We've just had a few centuries of bad PR."

"Demons…"

"Not exactly. We—well, I suppose I'm technically mixed—have been judged to be something because of how we look."

Lawrence purses his lips. "I'm sure I have no idea what that's like."

I sigh at him and hold up one snow-white hand. "I never really got it for being a Chicano. I'm undercover. Some kids at school thought I was adopted when they saw my mother."

He laughs.

"So what happened that's so strange?"

"Ever hear of 'spontaneous human combustion?'"

I shrug. "Outside the waiting area of the DMV? No."

"Alan and Ana Perez, both around my age, died in their bed last night. Nothing much left of them but teeth and ashes."

"Ouch."

He glances at me after stopping at a red light. "That's not entirely the strangest part. The bed burned completely, but the fire didn't eat through the floor nor did it damage much of anything else. If someone cleared out what's left of the bed, no one would suspect anything happened in here."

"As long as they had no sense of smell. But yeah, sounds like magic was involved."

"My thoughts exactly."

I stare at traffic for a few minutes, lost in thought. "Is there anyone out there who'd want to hurt them?"

"Not that the police have been able to find so far. The man was an accountant, his wife taught grade school. Got a detective still looking into it, but she hasn't found anything that might suggest a motive for murdering them. So far, they appear painfully normal."

"Hence, me."

"Yep."

A short ride later, he pulls over in front of a small house on Marvine Street. Other than a police cruiser sitting there, nothing appears out of the ordinary. The place has a tiny lawn with a single tree in it, so small it's barely worth buying a mower. Seriously, the patch of grass isn't much bigger than my bathroom at home.

The front door opens as we approach the small porch area, basically a sidewalk extension with some white metal fencing around it. A cop inside gives us a nod of welcome.

"Hey, how goes?" asks Lawrence.

"Quiet." The cop, Dressler, E according to his nameplate, shivers. "Creepy in here."

"Always does feel strange where people die." Lawrence moves past him, heading for a stairwell straight in front of the doorway.

Officer Dressler looks me up and down. I can practically see the crash occur in his head. He finds me simultaneously attractive but creepy due to my too-white complexion. The end result leaves him neutral—and not hitting on me, which I'm cool with. "Hey."

"Hey." I follow Lawrence upstairs.

A smell like fireplace wood smoke mixed with rotten grilled meat —ugh—hangs in the air on the second floor. It's also got a note of some other fragrance I can't identify, earthy and damp. The scent feels like it ought to be familiar but I'm drawing a blank.

Sooty footprints mark the beige rug near the master bedroom, though they're faint, not like a major fire happened. When I approach the door, I pick up on an odd energy in the air. It could be ghosts or magic lingering in the aftermath, but it isn't terribly strong.

Lawrence steps into the room first but moves aside to give me an unobstructed view. I stop in the doorway, not quite sure how to process the sight... or the smell. The ashes on the floor appear greasy, and have a rancid foul odor somewhere between carrion and spoiled dairy.

A queen-sized bed frame occupies the center of the opposite wall, the inside scorched black, the surfaces facing away from the bed unscathed. Only a few squiggly bits of metal remain of the box spring. A U-shaped strip of comforter sits on the floor around a burn mark, the sand-brown fabric slightly browned from smoke exposure but otherwise fairly normal. It looks like someone used a laser to cut the outermost six inches away from it on three sides.

Anything that had been in or on the bed became ash. Blackening marks the headboard and the wall behind it, up to a sooty patch where the rising smoke stained the ceiling. The window is open a little, screen intact, and the smear trail on the ceiling suggests the smoke went out that way.

"Was the window like that or did the guys open it when they put the fire out?" I ask.

Lawrence, hands on his hips, shakes his head. "Fire was already out before they got here. Neighbors saw the smoke in the morning and called it in. Best I can figure, the people who lived here probably ignited around eleven last night and the fire burned itself out before morning."

"So strange that the damage is this limited," I say, crouching by the corner of the bed.

"Well, the general theory of it is 'wick effect.' Body fat melts and burns like a candle, seeps into fabric and keeps going." Lawrence walks up to the left side of the bed, pointing. "That they died in their sleep aligns with prior cases of supposed spontaneous human combustion. Usually, the victims have limited mobility, but these people weren't elderly, obese, or handicapped."

I cringe at the idea of touching the ashes since they're so greasy and nasty smelling… but, they're my best chance for a psychic hit.

"Already ruled out external ignition sources." Lawrence gestures at the largely undamaged nightstand beside the bed. "No sign either one of them smoked, or even vaped. Also, doesn't seem like they suffered from alcoholism. Another thing that doesn't fit the usual profile for victims of spontaneous combustion."

"Right…" I clench my jaw and touch my fingertips to the ashes.

Ick. They're squishy.

I try to open my psychic 'feeler' for anything that might be out there to read. The darkness of my closed eyes gives way to a view as if I'm floating near the ceiling of this bedroom at night. It's too dark to see much, but a little bit of moonlight coming in the window reveals the shape of the deceased couple in bed. The silence breaks after a moment when the woman sits up and emits a pained gasp, smoke blowing out of her nostrils. Her husband twitches. She feebly tries to grab at her chest, but collapses flat on her back barely two seconds after sitting upright.

Something tells me they're already dead. If not for the smoke coming out of their noses, I'd have said they had simultaneous heart attacks. That would be pretty damn strange, too. Seconds later, orange glow radiates from inside their torsos, brighter at the stomach. Lawrence mentioned fat melting and burning, so that could explain the location of the glow. Ouch. I mean it's not like I can really sympathize with what it would feel like to burn, but the idea of having a creeping flame roving around under the skin still makes me squirm.

A few minutes after the woman sat up and gasped, a lick of flame emerges past the comforter. Smoke billows from her stomach like a scale model of a volcano about to blow. Fire spreads out along the fabric. The man's gut erupts in flame not long after, though neither one of them move. I glide closer, trying to get a better look. Based on the amount of smoke that blasted out of them when the skin ruptured, either that fire had been burning inside them for a while already, or it ignited with fury. The way that woman sat up makes me think sudden ignition and it either caused a heart attack from extreme pain or physically destroyed the heart. I can't imagine someone burning alive from the inside out and not feeling it. Though, maybe sleep paralysis had kicked in.

Ugh. What an awful thing to experience.

Flames spread over the bed, mostly confined to the area of the corpses, which burn like oil-soaked sponges. There's little for me to do but watch, and the vision ends once the entire bed is in full conflagration.

I come back to reality with Lawrence crouched beside me looking worried, the taste of smoke on my breath, and pain in my stomach.

"What?" I ask.

"You grabbed your chest like you had a heart attack. Please tell me that came from the psychic stuff."

"Yeah." I stand, eye the black stuff on my fingertips, and look around for somewhere to wipe it. Finding no good spot, I make for the bathroom in the hall. "They just ignited out of nowhere in the middle of the night."

While washing my hands, I explain what I saw in the vision.

"Damn. That's both what I wanted to hear and *not* what I wanted to hear."

"How's that?" I ask, reaching for the towel.

He chuckles. "Well, it doesn't sound like murder. Hopefully it's a one-off. But, it's still going to be a bear to determine the cause."

I glance at the sanitary pearl by the toilet. "Think the poop gem malfunctioned? The fire seemed like it started in their lower abdomen."

Lawrence squirms at the suggestion the magical cleaning device might've literally lit a fire under someone's ass. "I think they would've felt that and not gone to bed."

"I could see one of them waking up in the middle of the night to go and wandering back to bed half awake, but not both of them. Ignition occurred almost simultaneously. Just showed faster on her due to size. Or his went off more violently. He never even sat up."

"Hmm." Lawrence prods the pearl in the wall beside the toilet. A brief magical glow appears in the bowl, lingers a few seconds, and fades. "Looks normal, but I suppose it's a theory worth looking into. We'll have to contract out to an enchanter."

"Call my friend Natalie Diaz. She won't overcharge the FD." I smile.

Lawrence folds his arms and glances back toward the bedroom. "So, they just caught fire in the middle of the night."

"Looks that way."

"Well, I'll be damned. Always thought that spontaneous combustion thing was folklore. You *sure* this wasn't outside work?"

I shrug. "I'm not an expert on magic. I suppose it *could* be, but I didn't see or feel anything that made me suspect deliberate malice."

He sighs. "All right. Thanks for comin' out here."

"Not a problem. Happy to help whenever you need."

Lawrence pats me on the back. "You're a good soul, Brooklyn. Don't make the same mistake I did."

"What's that?" I raise an eyebrow.

He grins. "Don't grow old and cynical."

"Heh. No promises about the cynical part, but… Okay. I won't get old."

Lawrence's smile dies to a look of concern, like he's worried I'm going to die young. I let my horns out and smirk at him.

"Oh." He laughs. "Right."

# 6

## DESPERATE MEASURES

Ashley's standing outside my door when I arrive home a couple minutes after six that night. Her raspberry T-shirt and jean shorts look newish but still give off the 'thrift store' scent I remember all too well. Cheap purple glitter nail polish adorns her toes.

Taking the bus would've eaten a half hour of *my* time, so I flew home. Some of the guys complain the twelve-hour six-to-six shifts aren't for 'old men' (meaning anyone over twenty-five) but they don't really bother me. Especially since we're allowed to nap in the barracks if there's nothing that needs to be done at the station.

"Hey…" I look around. "Where's your mom?"

"She had to go somewhere."

I open my door, ushering her inside. "And she just left you standing out here in the hall?"

"Not allowed to be home alone yet." Ashley pads over to the couch and flops down.

Ugh. I need to talk to her. It's not exactly out on the street, but who leaves an eight-year-old standing around alone in a public hallway? The people in our building are okay, but this isn't the greatest part of town. Anyone could've walked in here. Eight or not, being home alone behind a locked door is still better than that... even with access to a stove and whatever chemicals are under the sink.

"She couldn't wait for me to get back? She didn't even text me."

"You always come home around six thirty. Mom said I'd be okay to wait a little bit. I didn't go inside 'cause you said I can't be here alone. If I saw someone scary, I'd go inside and pretend I was talking to you."

Sigh. I pat her on the head then stroll off to my bedroom. "That's fine. I just don't want you getting hurt."

Video game noises start up as I change out of my uniform. I stand there a moment considering clothing options before settling on a pair of sweat shorts and a BMO T-shirt. Back in college, I used to be a huge fan of Black Mage Orchestra, but for no particular reason haven't felt the urge to listen to them lately.

Ashley's settled in with her cartoon fox game, chasing glowing fruits and gems. She looks away from the screen long enough to grin at me as I cross to the kitchen. Hmm. Tonight's going to be Hamburger Minion with some taco seasonings.

I amuse myself by clawing up the ground beef instead of using a knife. The kid appears in the kitchen doorway a few minutes later.

"Oh, whew!" She overacts wiping sweat off her brow. "No rune oven."

I raspberry her.

She giggles and runs back to the game.

Eventually, food's done and she heads into the kitchen to join me at the table, swishing her feet back and forth while eating. This food's about as Mexican as borscht, but it's quick... and it goes over well with the kid. So well in fact that it takes me over ten minutes to pick up on something bothering her. It's the same look I probably had on my face when Mom had to go to work at night for her second shift. When I'd been little, she took me to the diner. Around nine or so, I started staying home alone. It really is a damn miracle I *didn't* blow up our house. Curious kid with minimal ability to resist temptation plus alone equals recipe for disaster.

Yet for whatever reason, I never did the pyromaniac thing as a kid, even though I find fire mesmerizing and beautiful now.

Ashley helps me with the dishes after, and we relocate to the sofa. She resumes her game while I sit on the phone with Jason. I kinda lose track of the clock until the kid runs to the bathroom for the third time. The food wasn't *that* bad. I glance at the phone and notice it's a few minutes past eleven at night.

"Huh, that's odd."

"What?" asks Jason.

"I just noticed the time. Ash's mother still isn't back yet. Usually, she walks her over and makes sure I'm here. Tonight, I found the kid in the hallway alone."

"Damn. You don't think she dropped her on you and ran off?"

That I'm not initially freaked out at that thought worries me. Okay, maybe the kid's grown on me somewhat, but it would crush her to be abandoned by her mom. Also, between my schedule and other complications of a supernatural persuasion, I'm not sure a kid's a great idea for me now. I'd probably ask Mom to take her in. Though, in all honestly, social services would grab her and either Mom and I would have to jump through a million hoops and probably still wouldn't get her. Grr.

But... I also don't think Tracy would do that.

"That doesn't feel right. Ash looked a little gloomy over dinner. Maybe she knows something." The toilet flushes. "Let me sort this out? Call you... probably tomorrow."

"Okay, babe. Stay safe."

"I'll try."

We kiss at the phone and hang up. I'm half tempted to suggest he put in for a permanent transfer to my station house. The week or so he filled in for Baker going out on vacation was nice. Though, if we ever get serious, maybe it would be better that he stay at another house. Spending all day at work with him then all night at home with him might drive one or both of us nuts.

Ashley pads back in and scoots onto the couch. She yawns, staring at the controller as if trying to make up her mind about playing more or just curling up and taking a nap.

"Hey, kiddo. It's pretty late."

"Yeah." She yawns again.

"What time is your mom supposed to get back?"

She shrugs. "Didn't say."

I don't get any sense of worry from her that she's afraid her mother *won't* come back. That's good. I call Tracy, but the connection goes straight to voicemail, not even one ring. Either her phone's out of a coverage area, off, or she's put it on do-not-disturb.

"She was on the phone with that guy again."

"What guy?" I ask.

"The same guy I told you about a couple days ago. F-Bomb. He used to live next door and sold drugs."

I let my head fall back against the couch. "Ugh. That's not good." I mean, slightly hypocritical of me, but one: I wasn't a junkie, and two: I didn't have a kid to take care of while experimenting. Technically, I *was* a kid at the time. Now that I think about it, I probably cheated. My not-quite-human body might not even be able to become addicted to stuff. Then again, I didn't touch anything hard core. Just the 'fun' drugs.

"Mom didn't take any drugs, but she sometimes did stuff for the guy an' got money for it. I don't 'member too much 'cause I was little then."

"You're little now." I poke her in the side.

She manages a weak smile. "I'm scared she got hurt. She should be home already."

"Let's check around your place. Maybe I can find something or get a hit on where she went."

Ashley yawns. "Hit? You mean drugs?"

"No." I tap my head. "Psychic hit."

"Oh!" She seems to wake back up. "Okay. Don't kick the door this time, okay?"

"I won't." A slow mental sigh rolls over my brain. How much does she remember or understand about what Frank wanted to do to her? Other than some nightmares, she's barely shown any reaction to it—and hasn't mentioned him once except for saying I threw 'a man' out a window the last time I looked angry.

Ashley gets up and leads me out into the hall, one door to the right. She unlocks it with the second key on the string around her neck. The place looks pretty much the same as I remember, only without broken glass all over the floor and a pervert on the couch. Tracy's even neatened the place up a bit.

I roam around touching random objects while concentrating on reading them. Ashley shadows me for a little while, but eventually wanders off to her bedroom and crawls in under the covers clutching her enchanted faerie toy. Her room is sparse like mine was at that age. Not too much decoration beyond crayon drawings. All the toys— other than Vy the faerie—look well-worn, clearly hand-me-downs or stuff from the thrift store.

My mother got lucky. I didn't care much about toys, being more of a 'go out and get dirty' type kid. Ash is more of a 'girly-girl' than I ever was. Now I'm getting the itch to play Santa. Meh. Later. With the kid out cold, I resume searching the apartment, deciding to hit Tracy's room next.

The clothes she wears to nursing school are isolated from everything else in a separate closet while the majority of her wardrobe exists in floor piles. A beat-up white chest of drawers along one wall holds enough beauty products to stock a CVS. The mirror hung over it doesn't have any incriminating Post-It notes, nor do I receive any visions from touching it.

A nasty one of Frank slapping the shit out of Tracy hits me when I touch the bed itself, but I break out of it and wobble back a few steps. The laptop on her small computer desk doesn't give me a full-on vision, but I pick up a strong sense of sadness and worry. It's not to the point I become concerned she might hurt herself, more that she's overwhelmed with life. For no particular reason, I start thinking about money, specifically not having enough. Ahh. That must be coming from Tracy. Makes sense.

Peeking under the bed reveals a grey shoebox. I pull it out and lift the lid to find two dildos, a collar, and two pairs of handcuffs. Nope. Not touching any of that. I do, however, gawk at the pink one, cringing at the size of it. Wow. Everyone always complains about unrealistic body images for girls, but that thing sets a standard no man alive could meet... and I'm not sure who would want to. Babies are supposed to go *out.*

Shudder.

Beneath the 'tools,' a plastic baggie holds a smattering of small blue pills. Probably E. Or maybe faerie dust. I'm tempted to... no. Still don't want to touch that. Even looking at this box is prying a bit too far into her personal life. A psychic read from this shit would be way beyond. See, right here I know I fail at being a demon. I probably should scoop up every dark secret I can find to use as leverage over her later on—but that's not who I am.

Right. Kids have the strangest sixth sense about walking in at bad moments. Before that happens here, I cover the box and push it back under the bed. A suspicious dent in the drywall draws my attention. Touching it provides a brief vision of flying face first into the wall. I wake up flat on my back upon the floor, gripped by a few seconds of pure fear that this is the moment Frank will kill me.

Of course, it's not my fear. It's lingering from the vision.

Ooh. If it's possible to have negative remorse for killing someone, I do. Almost makes me want that whole Hell myth to be true so I can wish Frank went there. Given all the screaming and banging from this apartment that used to annoy me, it's probably pointless to touch any dents or holes. They're all likely to be the same thing. It's also not like someone barged into the place and kidnapped her. Signs of violence here wouldn't be related to her current situation, whatever it may be.

I stick my head into the bathroom for a cursory look around and wind up staring at a used sanitary pad in the wastebasket. Blood. Oh, now there's a question that would make Dad squirm. Can *that* blood be used for the tracking magic? One way to find out.

After fishing the thing out of the basket, I stare into the dark crimson stain and concentrate the same way Dad showed me. My brain wobbles like a gelatin mold, and I have the strangest sense the bloodstain on the cotton moves back and forth. A few seconds later, it glows dark orange and falls inward, becoming a tunnel with shifting, fiery sides. Sure enough, I get a sense of direction.

Great. I can find Tracy.

Crap. I can't leave Ashley here alone.

I jog back to my apartment, grab my phone, and call Natalie.

"Oh hey. What's up? Bit late for you to be awake?"

Her obvious joke makes me laugh. I'm not sure if she's making fun of me for getting so little sleep lately or because I'd always been a night owl. Go figure I wind up with a job that requires me to be at the 'office' by six in the morning. "Something's up with Tracy. I can't get in touch with her and she didn't come back. Can I drop the kid off at your place for a little while? Don't want to leave her alone."

"Sure. No problem."

"Cool. Be there soon."

I fling off the sweat shorts for black jeans, and hurriedly put on my boots before activating Natalie's amulet to 'store' the clothes and replace them with the illusory 'sparkle goth' getup. It's beyond strange to feel naked but look dressed. Still, my wings won't rip illusions apart. I jog back to Tracy's apartment, bundle Ashley in her blanket and carry her to the roof.

She wakes up as soon as we step outside. "Mmm… where are we?"

"It's okay, Ash. You can go back to sleep. I'm going to go look for your mom, but first, I gotta bring you to Natalie's place."

"Oh, cool." She reaches one arm out of the blanket cocoon and sorta-hugs me.

Cradling her to my chest, I let the wings out and jump airborne. Flying wakes her up and she spends the whole few-minute flight to Natalie's shop gawking in awe at the ground below. I swoop down for a landing in the back yard.

"Can I go swimming?" asks Ashley.

"It's after eleven at night, and cold."

"Not that cold." She grins. "You're always cold."

"Okay, fair point. But it's too dark to swim." I hurry up onto the deck and knock on the sliding glass.

Natalie appears with a confused expression until she notices my wings are out. She runs over and pulls the door aside. "What's the situation?"

"Not sure yet." I set Ashley down on her feet, still mostly bundled in her blanket, then hold up the sanitary pad in my left hand. "Got a blood trace on her."

"Eww!" Natalie cringes.

"What? You sound like a guy. It's only blood. It's not like corrosive or contaminated."

"I know, but it's someone *else's*."

"Your point? Not like I'm tasting it."

She gags.

I point at her. "Gotcha."

"So foul." She shakes her head at me, then chuckles.

"Okay. I'll be back as soon as I can."

*Hopefully with good news.*

# 7

## LESSER EVILS

Shit.

A few minutes into the process of flying toward the pull the magic is giving me from the blood, it occurs to me that the warmongers might be involved. They have to know Laniah warned me about an attempt to grab my mother, so they could've gone after Tracy instead. That makes even less sense to me than Mom.

I mean, I kinda like Tracy as a friend, but a 'destroy the world or we kill her' situation is a no brainer. Sorry girl, take one for 'team humanity' there. Also, if those morons had anything to do with Tracy, I'm sure they would've made contact with me by now. No, I can't help but think this is all her doing. Desperate for money, phone call from a dealer she used to know… she's probably been talked into something stupid in hopes of quick cash.

Flying naked is not the most comfortable thing once I get going at a decent speed. Flappage. My chest isn't exactly epic, but wind shear does bizarre things to fat-filled skin pouches. Illusory clothing doesn't help at all to keep things in place, so I armor up. I seem to gain a fair amount of speed once I've fully shifted, and I barely notice the breeze anymore—like wearing a motorcycle helmet on my everything.

Traveling in a straight line is definitely easier than sitting in the car while guiding Emerson around in search of zombies. No going in circles trying to figure out where to turn, and even his souped-up police sedan can't touch my top speed.

In minutes, the sense leading me whips by and starts pulling me backward. That means I just shot straight over her. Nice! She's not far off. I slow and wheel around in a turn, following the tracking magic to a construction site in northwest Philly. From the size of it, looks like it's going to be either a hotel or corporate office tower whenever they finish it. Presently, the building is little more than a stack of concrete slabs with completely open walls covered in plastic sheeting.

Tracy and some guy I've never seen before squeeze through the fence. They sprint across the open dirt, running past piles of building materials and piping, heading for the ground floor under the glare of a spotlight from a helicopter. Nine police cars, all lights and sirens, arrive in a swarm near both access gates to the property.

Oh, shit, Tracy. What the hell did you do? Something tells me the guy with her is F-Bomb.

Hesitation lasts only a few seconds before I decide to help. My history of messing with cops is long and legendary, no sense breaking tradition now. Except for being old enough for jail. Bah. Okay, first order of business: the helicopter. I fly off enough to get a 'running' start and approach the heli from behind at probably 350 miles an hour.

I buzz the chopper as close as I can get without hitting it, and swipe out with my tail blade at the electronics pod near the nose. The spotlight dies in time with a shower of sparks erupting behind me. I don't look back, heading around the corner of the building-in-progress before the pilot can whirl the bird around in search of what hit him.

The *crash* of the electronics pod striking the ground sets off a flurry of shouting from the cops below. No more searchlight... and probably infrared as well. Damn sure better not get caught after that. That stuff was probably expensive. Cops on the ground gather around the fallen pod, some stand guard at the gates. Cool. I have some time —not much, but some is better than none.

For stealth, I change back to normal. It's easier to hide being two feet shorter, not to mention the illusory clothing is black. I do, however leave the wings out since flying is faster than stairs. Two floors down from where I'm hovering, Tracy scrambles across a wide-open section of floor and crawls into the beginnings of a ventilation duct. No idea where the guy went, but I don't really care.

I rip past the plastic, slip into the building and land nearby, startled at the pat of my bare feet on concrete when I appear to be wearing boots. Wow, magic is weird. When I reach the opening, I crouch down on one knee. Tracy's cowering inside like a frightened child hiding from the closet monster.

"Come on," I whisper. "We gotta get out of here."

Tracy blinks at me in grateful surprise. Grinning, she scrambles out of the vent. I back off so she can stand, and grab her arm. "W-what are you gonna do?"

"No time to explain. Cops won't be able to find us. Did they see you?"

"I-I don't think so. I mean, not my face."

I drag her to the edge. "Good."

"Wait." She pulls back. "We can't leave Rob."

"Oh. Thought that was F-Bomb."

She emits a nervous laugh. "Same dude. He just went by that on the street. Only an idiot uses his real name to sell drugs."

"Only an idiot winds up running from half the cops in Philly. Who is this guy, and what the F-Bomb did you step in?" I peer over the side at the wavering flashlight beams a couple stories below us.

She clings to my arm, shaking in fear. "I used to know him back home. He sold shit, but things aren't going too well for him. He kinda pressured me into helping him rob a pawn shop. The dude screwed him over and he wanted his shit back, plus whatever cash he could grab."

"Screw him. Hop on my back."

"But..." She moves around behind me and grabs on. "If we leave him behind, he'll rat me out."

"Why would he? What could he gain from it?"

"Just to be an asshole. He's like that. Rob wouldn't go down alone. It would piss him off to get nailed for something someone else got away with. And if he gets away, he's gonna do it again. Said he's got some video of me that'll make them take Ashley."

I glance back at her. "You think he's full of shit?"

"Umm." She shrugs. "Probably. Other than getting high a couple times, I didn't really ever do anything that bad. And I didn't have Ash when I used to get wasted."

"Do you like this guy?"

The tromping and scuffing of police shoes echoes out of the stairwell.

"Uhh." She swallows hard. "Not really. He was just less shitty to hang around with than the people who left me alone because I hung out with him. I grew up in a really bad part of town. Gangs everywhere."

Tracy's throwing off too much guilt. "He gave you some shit, didn't he?"

"Umm." She fidgets. "Mostly offered money… I don't make a lot. But, yeah, he gave me some shit. I haven't taken it. Don't plan to."

I sigh. "Hold on tight."

When she squeezes me, I jump off the edge, swing around, and fly up another four stories.

"Holy fuck," rasps Tracy. "You're really flying."

Since I no longer need it, I… *don't* drop the sanitary pad. Just my luck, the cops will find the damn thing and somehow manage to use her blood to find us. Or one of their psychics will sniff me out because I used magic through it. Can't just toss it. Gotta destroy it. We stand there in total silence for a few seconds as I scan the mostly empty floor. Pretty sure my ears told me Rob would be on this level, or maybe higher. Finally, I spot a shadow move near the opposite side of the building. The dealer's fast-walking to the left, heading for another stairwell.

Need a little more size and bulk, I think.

Grinning, I full shift, the increase in my height lifting Tracy off her feet. She bites back a startled scream but doesn't let go. I lean forward into a jog, heading right at him. He sees me and stops short with a terrified open-mouthed stare seconds before I crash into him, flinging him off the—probably twenty-seventh—story.

"Oops," I deadpan. "Sorry, dude."

He plummets straight down, screaming.

I power climb, Tracy dangling off me like a human cloak. A cluster of flashlights appears at the edge of the building, pointing down. She emits as much of a shriek as she can out her nose, trying to keep quiet. Even if she'd yelled at full volume, the cops wouldn't have noticed. We're already a good distance away from the property. In fact, I didn't even hear Rob go splat. Tracy drops about forty whispered F-bombs in a row, then goes quiet for the few minutes it takes me to find a nice, high roof on a nearby office tower, a decent place to stop for a chat.

Upon landing, I shift back to normal and wind up wearing a bra of hands.

"Uhh… why do you feel naked?" asks Tracy, squeezing my breasts in an 'am I feeling what I think I'm feeling' kind of way.

"Because I am." I pluck her hands away and activate the amulet to re-summon my clothes. The frilly black outfit with excessive lace and skull brocade trades places with my BMO tee and jeans. "Now, I'm not. Magic amulet. Much easier to let the wings out."

"That's fucked up." She looks me up and down. "But not as fucked up as you just killing Rob."

"He was trying to get you hooked and dependent." I fold my arms. "What did he give you?"

Tracy looks down and pulls a small plastic baggie out of her pocket with white powder in it.. "Little H."

I tap my boot.

"Look, I wasn't gonna take the shit. I know exactly what he was trying to do. I'm not stupid."

"Says the woman who just helped a dude break into a pawn shop."

She smirks at me. "You're one to talk. Hear you got a record longer than mine. Like ten times."

"Heh. Yeah, but it's all kid bullshit. Worst thing I ever did was steal a car and joyride. Didn't keep the thing."

"Worst thing you ever did was kill Rob."

I examine my fingernails. "Accident."

"Bullshit."

"So? The guy was taking advantage of you. You said he would've ratted you out, and you don't really like him. He would've been a threat to you and Ashley."

I toss the sanitary pad to the ground.

"The heck?" asks Tracy. "Do I even want to know why you're carrying a used pad around?"

"It's how I found you." I raise a hand toward it and blast it with Imbreleth fire.

"Gah!" Tracy jumps back. "You're a mage?"

"Nope. We had this conversation already."

"Oh." She bites her lip. "Right. Sorry. Little out of it right now."

"If you wanna drop that junk I can toast it, too. Get rid of the evidence."

"I'm not gonna take it. Might try to sell it though. Need the money. School is so damn expensive."

I sigh. "And what if you get busted? What happens to Ashley?"

She glances at me.

"Not that I really give a shit about you selling drugs, but is it worth the risk? What's that baggie worth? Maybe fifty bucks?"

"Not even that much." She tosses it on the black scorch mark that used to be a pad. "And knowing Rob, it's probably tainted anyway... or cut so thin it won't even do anything."

I nuke it. She stares at the spot like a kid who just had their favorite toy confiscated. It's not the needy longing of an addict, more like someone teasing a homeless guy with a $50 bill.

"Come on..." I full shift, letting the amulet auto-grab my clothes to interdimensional safety. "Little safer if I carry you up front."

"Is it?" She walks closer.

"Yeah." I scoop her up in my arms, sideways like a bride about to go over the threshold. "This way, you won't fall and die if your arms get tired."

She gulps.

# 8

## DEPENDENT

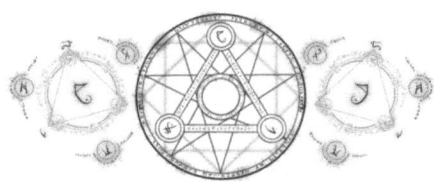

We cruise in the direction I think leads to Natalie's shop.

Wonder if Garmin makes a wearable? My phone's stashed away in my pocket in another plane of existence, so I can't exactly check it. Tracy's silent for a while, but too frightened to look around. She keeps her eyes clamped shut, hands together at her chin. Guess in her position, I'd be kinda scared, too. Somewhere between being a thousand feet in the air and in the grip of an entity who blithely killed a guy, she could be wondering how easily I could grow bored and drop her on purpose.

I hope she knows me better than that. Yeah, I'm like three-quarters Shaar'Nath, and they, too, kinda regard humans as insignificant. *I* don't. At least not all humans. Only some of them.

"Sorry," says Tracy. "I fucked up. Holy shit, thank you for getting me out of there."

"Pure luck."

"Luck?" She risks opening one eye to look up at my face. "You came looking for me on purpose. How is that luck?"

"That I got there when I did. Those cops would've had you in another few minutes."

She gulps. "We'd been running for like two hours. Spent a while hiding in this other abandoned building, but Rob couldn't play it cool. When we felt safe enough to leave, a cop saw us and he got spooked."

I shake my head. "Sprinting away the instant you see a cop is about the dumbest thing possible. Might as well confess that you did something."

"Yeah."

Aha! I recognize the area. Guess I *can* find Kensington from the sky at night. The wedge-shaped building with Nat's favorite coffee shop catches my eye. Though after dealing with nazedeh, a place called ReAnimator Coffee kinda worries me. Okay, time for a talk. I land on the roof of the coffee shop and set Tracy down on her feet.

"What's this?" She looks around.

"My friend's store is just down the street a bit. Just wanted to make sure you had your head on straight before we pick Ash up. I know it's kinda weird coming from me, but there are better ways to survive than crime."

"Yeah, I know." She kicks at the roof, looking down.

"You have a decent shot with nursing school. Don't throw that away. You get busted for some bullshit, they'll never let you become an RN. If you're gonna break the law, go big. Go 'never have to work again and run to Mexico' big. Wait, maybe not Mexico. Quetzalcoatls suck. Mom told me about those damn things. Flying snakes the size of telephone poles."

Tracy blinks at me. "Are you messing with me?"

"Not intentionally. Mom might've been pulling my leg. Just don't do dumb shit, okay?"

"I dunno. It's too much damn pressure. I'm so worried about affording rent and food and stuff. No idea when I'm supposed to study or do any homework while working fifty hours a week or more. I love Ashley more than anything, but I wasn't ready to have a kid yet. She surprised me, and Keith fucked off and left us as soon as I told him I was pregnant. I don't even know what state he's in now. I have no idea how to be a mother or raise a kid. My parents barely knew I existed."

"Trace..."

She looks up at me.

"Two ancient races of extraplanar creatures made me—well, arranged my birth—to destroy the entire world. Some of them want to kill me to prevent me from doing that. Some of them want to do whatever they can to force me to destroy the universe. Balancing school and a job doesn't seem like much pressure compared to that."

"Heh." She swipes her hair off her face. "Yeah, I guess. But I'm also not a half… whatever."

"My mom worked her ass off to support me when I was a kid. She didn't have any real job skills either. She waited tables. It's not fun, but it is possible, and I know you can do it. For the next ten years, you've got a little person entirely dependent on you not to fuck up and get dead or wind up in jail."

She blinks, stares at me for a few seconds, then bursts into tears while sinking to sit on the roof.

Ugh. Not the reaction I was hoping for.

I sit next to her. "Hey… You know I'm willing to help if you need me to. Happy to watch her whenever I can. Or, if I'm at work, my mother will take her. I know you agreed to help that guy tonight because you're trying to do the best you can for Ash and needed the money. Desperation sucks balls." I raise an eyebrow. "Sometimes literally, but I'm not suggesting you turn tricks."

She laughs, wiping her eyes.

"You've got a couple tough years, but once you're out of school, you get a job as a nurse and you'll be golden."

Tracy sighs. "They don't make that much. Especially not right out of school."

"Yeah, but it's more than the coffee shop, right?"

"Okay, yeah, that's true."

"Look, what I'm trying to say here is, you're not facing this shit alone. I'm here. Nat, too. And if things get bad, we can call in the big guns."

"Big guns?" She blinks. "What, like a demon army?"

"No, my mother." I grin. "Though, I could probably swing the demon army if I ask nicely enough."

"Now you're messing with me."

I elbow her in the side. "Actually, I'm being serious. My dad has some pull. But... unless you've got like an entire street gang trying to kill you, I don't see them being much help."

Tracy takes a few deep breaths and composes herself. "Okay. Well, it's not like I have to worry about Rob talking me into any stupid shit again seeing as how you threw him off a building."

"Oops," I deadpan. "Oh, did the pawn shop have any video?"

She shrugs. "No idea. We didn't even get inside. Dumbass set off the alarm. He couldn't get the door open so he smashed a window. Couple of guard dogs appeared in a patch of glowing light, so we ran like hell."

"Cool. No video." I stand and pull her up. "Time to go. It's way past your kid's bedtime."

After a short hop to the ground, I put the wings away. We cross the street and head down to the next corner where Natalie's shop, Enchanted Evenings, sits. The lights are still on inside, and Natalie's barely awake in one of the seats by the play area.

Peeking in the window, I telekinetically flip the deadbolt to open the door, and go inside. The magical chimes wake Natalie, and she flails around in a disoriented scramble, pointing a wand at me. Fortunately, she realizes who I am before activating it.

"Crap, Brook..." She huffs. "You know they have this thing called knocking?"

"Sorry. Not my nature." I wink. "Where's the kidling?"

Natalie points at the play area.

"Wow, she's still up? It's after midnight." I approach the waist-high wooden wall enclosing it, but fail to spot any sign of child. "Umm. She's gone."

"Train," says Natalie.

A sizable toy trainset sprawls out on the floor a few feet in from the swinging saloon-style gate, its path weaving around the shelves and displays. The track sections and the train itself are all made of wood painted in bright colors, so it's quite obviously magical in nature since its moving. Ashley, all four inches of her, leans out the 'window' of the engine and cheers.

Tracy appears to spot her the same moment I do—and nearly faints. She babbles at me, unable to form coherent words.

"It's fine." I step into the play area and hit the stop gem on the control board with my foot.

Ashley hops off the train and runs for the dollhouse. I grin to myself, thinking of making a joke that Natalie shrank her so it costs less to feed her, but bite it back. Don't want the kid feeling guilty about existing.

"What happened to her?" blurts Tracy. "She's..."

A doorbell ring comes from the dollhouse, and Ashley grows back to normal size in a swirl of pink-purple light. Uh oh. She's hit 'Stage Three.' She's gone past being exhausted to hyper. I can almost see her eyeballs vibrating. Overtired children are way worse than caffeinated kids... at least if my past is any indication.

"Mom!" She zooms over and jumps into a koala hug, somehow managing to cheer and cry at the same time. "I was so scared."

Despite the guilt on Tracy's face, I still hit her with a 'see what I mean' stare. She squeezes her daughter, rubbing a hand up and down the girl's back while mumbling reassuring things. The intent radiating from her is pretty clear. I don't think she's going to risk breaking the law again.

At least, not unless she can retire off whatever she steals in one shot.

# 9

## UNDER THE BUS

Ugh.

Just like Ashley, I think I've hit stage three, too. I'm too wired to sleep between wondering how my mother is doing and playing chicken with a police helicopter. Bet there's some interesting stories going around the PD now. With any luck, they'll assume Rob slipped or maybe jumped on purpose.

I walk straight past my apartment after a good night hug from Ashley and a long teary thank you from Tracy. On the short walk to Kwan's Market, I feel a few eyes on me from the shadows, but I don't really care.

The place is its usual retina-destroying bright white. I swear this guy has stock in the company that makes LED light tubes. Honestly, I have no idea *why* I'm here. Just something I always seem to do when I feel restless. The donut selection at 12:28 a.m. is pretty crappy. All the ones still in the case are there for reasons, not the least of which is that they've been in that case since six this morning.

Hmm. I'm not going to *try* to stay up all night, so no coffee. A bag of white cheddar jalapeno popcorn catches my eye. That'll do. I grab it and head back down the aisle toward the register right as a guy in a ski mask runs in and shoves a small handgun in Mr. Kwan's face.

Good grief. Seriously? Again?

I walk up behind the guy as if on line. "Wow. Another one?"

The dude's all sorts of twitchy. He nearly jumps over the counter into Kwan's arms at my sudden appearance. Somehow, he manages the self-control necessary to keep the weapon pointed at the owner instead of shooting me. "Back off, lady."

"Uhh," says Mr. Kwan in a shaky voice. "Are you going to kill this one, too?"

"I didn't technically kill the last guy. He survived the bus hitting him." I wag the popcorn at him and toss it on the counter. "If he's just going to stand there with a gun, would you mind?"

The guy with the ski mask jumps back and points his gun at me. "G-gimme the money."

"You're talking to the wrong person," I say. "I can't open the register."

Mr. Kwan gestures at me. "Not that man. The other one. He shot himself in the head when you looked at him."

"Fuckin, what?" The man points the gun back and forth between me and Kwan.

"Sorry," I say. "Should I make this guy shoot himself in the balls instead?"

"I have a goddamn gun," screams the guy, "stop fuckin' ignoring me!"

Mr. Kwan's sweating like a fiend, but keeps a stoic face.

I tilt my head as if listening to something, and open the door with a telekinetic poke. "I think I hear a bus coming."

The man jumps, screams, and whirls, aiming at the entrance. "That goddamned door just moved on its own."

"Yeah. I had to open it before I can throw you under the bus— literally. Don't want to break Mr. Kwan's door. Glass is expensive."

He spins around again, but before he can shove his gun up my nose, I hammer him in the face hard enough to knock him flat and send him sliding all the way to the door. Blood gushes down from his nose over his mouth.

I pull the bag open and toss a few pieces of popcorn in my mouth. "You can call the cops now. And what do I owe you for the popcorn?"

Mr. Kwan leans over the counter, peering at the unconscious gangbanger. "Is he dead?"

"Nah. Just out." I keep munching. "Why do you get robbed so damn much?"

"Uhh... only place open within like three miles at this hour. Maybe I should lock the doors at midnight."

I swipe my AATM crystal over the reader after he rings up the popcorn. "Or at least buy an anti-firearm enchantment."

"It'd cost me less to be robbed." He pushes the alarm button.

"My friend's an enchanter. She doesn't overcharge." I toss a few more bits of popcorn in my mouth while glancing at the door. Might as well stick around and talk to the police this time. Need to balance out my karma for breaking their helicopter.

Right. Cover story... been sitting around home all night watching TV, got the munchies.

# 10

## FIGURES... TUESDAY

A few long-ass days go by with nothing out of the ordinary going on.

Constant worry about my mother turns minutes into hours and has me jumping every time a phone rings. On one hand, I do appreciate nothing bad happening, but the calm makes me even more nervous. As far as I know, Laniah is still keeping an eye on her—somehow. I've called Mom every day, but she's never mentioned her, so maybe there's some Elestari magic stuff going on. Anyway, I think my mother is starting to get a little frustrated with me for pestering her.

Friday after work, Jason took me out to dinner and we spent the rest of the night at his place. It took me a little while to set aside my worry and get in the mood, but we eventually had fun.

The weekend was nice, until tragedy struck.

And by that, I mean Tuesday.

Specifically, my alarm going batshit at 5 a.m., playing the death knell for the weekend passed.

I drag myself out of bed, barely manage to resist the urge to smash the clock into bits, and take a shower. That done, I trudge to the kitchen and toss an egg burrito into the rune oven, then flick on the

TV. There still hasn't been anything on the news about a random attack on a police helicopter, so I'm guessing they've either decided to chalk it up as 'stuff too weird to talk about' or it's an active investigation. Then again, I might've just given fuel to the legend of the Seventeenth Street Pigeon.

Mean bastard... but it's a myth—I think.

The oven pings. As soon as I open the door, I realize I've been betrayed again. A chorizo-and-egg burrito should not smell like s'mores. A few pokes with a fork fails to cause a detonation of slime or the summoning of a minor demonic being, so I risk taking a bite.

Okay, that's weird. It has the consistency of eggs and sausage bits, but tastes like chocolate and marshmallows. Whatever. The rune oven has mutilated food worse than this before, at least the flavor combination works. Not like the banana-pickle atrocity.

This much chocolate this early in the morning requires coffee. With the burrito dangling from my teeth, I brew a single serving amount while trying to hold off on eating until it's ready.

"Authorities continue to investigate a bizarre event in upstate New York where six men all suffered lightning strikes over a period of ten minutes. Of the two survivors, one remains comatose. The names of the victims have not yet been released as authorities have not yet notified all families involved," says the reporter on the TV.

Whoever—or whatever—is out there going nuts with lightning isn't being subtle. Pretty sure the gas pipe fire, that chemical plant, and this new thing are all related despite the distance between the sites. Not like it's my problem to worry about, though. At least not until Lawrence asks me to investigate that gas line fire. Assuming they reopen that case.

I take a giant swig of coffee then another bite of overwhelming chocolate. Wonder if the rune oven is trying to offer me a bribe not to replace it? That thought makes me smile as I finish eating, kill the TV, and head to the bedroom to throw my uniform on.

Trying to lay low for a few days after the helicopter thing, I hop on a PEPTA bus as usual. Pretty sure there are a few creatures out there with bladed appendages sharp enough to slice steel, but I'd rather avoid suspicion entirely. So, I'm going to be Lucy Normal for a little while. People notice the uniform and offer pleasant smiles of greeting. Yeah, hi. That's it, nothing unusual here. No you're not sitting across the aisle from an extraplanar being with the power to destroy the world. Nope. Just little ol' me.

Head down, I almost nap, biting back a few chocolate-flavored burps. Oh, crap. Did that rune oven slip me a Trojan burrito? Is it going to do something bad to me? Wait, it's technically still chorizo... could just be the spice.

The bus falls abnormally quiet on the third stop from where I boarded. No one's getting on or off, but the driver hasn't pulled back out into traffic. Crap. Did the cops find me that fast?

I peer up and do a double take at a huge green bird standing at the head of the aisle next to the driver. It's somewhere between chicken and ostrich with a long, purple neck, bright green feathers, and big goofy eyes that don't quite point in the same direction.

Everyone around me has stopped moving, all gazing into space.

Oh, shit. That's a goddamned cockatrice. I ease up out of my seat and look around at an entire bus full of paralyzed people, including the driver. I sigh, staring at the enormous bird. Well, that's good to know... apparently, its mesmerizing magic doesn't work on me.

"Dammit. You're going to make me late."

It takes a step down the aisle, twisting its head side to side as if it can only focus one of its eyes on me at a time. Never saw a cockatrice up close before, so I'm not sure if they all look like this or if someone walloped this guy over the head with a bat and made him cross-eyed. Maybe it's confused about why I'm not paralyzed. This is not a good way to blend in, being the only one here still in possession of all their faculties.

Still, I don't want to be late.

"Shoo!" I say, heading toward it.

The five-foot-tall critter just stands there ogling me as I approach. It's mostly all legs and neck with a body not much bigger than a turkey on the upper end of large. Since it doesn't move, I grab and lift/shove it down the stairs to the sidewalk before shutting the door.

Looks like the eight or so people at the bus stop who'd been waiting to get on are also staring into the eighth dimension.

I twist around to frown at the stupefied bus driver. Dammit. How long does this shit take to wear off? And for that matter, how the hell did a cockatrice get past the shield around the city? Figures. Every time the Corporatists get power, they siphon money away from important shit and send it into someone's pocket. Bet the maintenance contract with the mages lapsed. I should be a bitch and fly this giant stupefying chicken straight to the governor's mansion.

Natalie answers the phone in nine rings, her voice a little raspy. "Hey Brook. Wow, you're up early. I'm still in bed."

"Sorry. I need your help dealing with a five-foot cock. It's too much for me to handle alone."

She coughs. "W-what?"

When I stop laughing, I say, "How long does paralysis from giant cock exposure last?"

She giggles.

"Sorry, couldn't resist. A cockatrice got on the bus this morning and everyone's a statue. How long does its effect last?"

"Oh. Ha. Not fair teasing the half-awake girl with a line like that. Gimme a sec."

"Okay."

Shuffling and muttering come over the line for a minute or two before she returns. "About an hour, but it can vary based on if the cockatrice was excited."

"Umm. I don't think he wants to mate with anyone." I bend to the side trying to peek at its undercarriage. "I don't even know if it's a boy. Wait... chickens aren't obvious like dogs. How do you tell?"

She sighs. "Not that kind of excited. Like scared or angry. They constantly radiate magic, but it hits harder if they're agitated."

"You do realize you used 'harder' in the same context as a five-foot cock, right?"

"I'm going back to bed." She raspberries me. "Unless you need something else."

"Any way to break someone out of it early?"

Natalie starts to say something but it mutates into a yawn. "Yeah. But nothing you can do. Requires magic."

"Okay. Guess I'm walking. Thanks."

"No problem."

I stash the phone in my pocket, hop off the bus, and walk past the confused giant chicken. A small group of pedestrians have started to collect on the sidewalk, forming a rather clear illustration of the outer limits of the creature's magical aura. It's kinda funny to see people walking along and just stop cold in their tracks with bewildered expressions.

Damn. So much for being subtle. I slip out of the crowd and head into the nearest alley, use the amulet to protect my clothes, and jump into the air like a dragon-winged goth fairy from hell. I mean, I'm grateful to Natalie for making this amulet. It's *such* a help. But she did kinda overdo the illusory clothing's frilliness a tad. The fluffy, layered black dress makes me look like an enormous porcelain doll. But, whatever.

From the air, the ring of open sidewalk around the cockatrice is even more obvious. Grr. Part of me feels guilty just leaving. Least I can do is call 911 and report it. Hazardous creature handling is not my job.

It's actually one of the few things that *doesn't* wind up going to the fire department.

Unless a dragon's involved.

And ugh. My 'Monday' starts off with a cockatrice strolling onto the bus. That's not a good portend.

# 11

## FOOM

Within minutes of me arriving at the station, I'm right back out the door with everyone's Starbucks requests. Works for me. I will never say no to free coffee. At one point, the guys designated me as the 'coffee fetcher' due to my being the newest one here. When Lamar showed up, I continued getting the coffee most likely due to being the only woman. Or maybe because I just never bothered to complain about it when they kept sending me.

Still, if I go get it, everyone adds a little extra money to cover my order. Not a bad deal.

Two cops in the Starbucks ahead of me on line chat about some unknown creature attacking a police chopper last week. I can't help myself.

"No shit? Any idea what it was or what made it attack?" I ask. "Heard someone say the Seventeenth Street Pigeon came out of hiding."

They look back at me, note my uniform, and wind up shaking their heads.

"Who knows?" asks the guy on the left, a big bald dude named Brinneman. "Sometimes those critters get confused by aircraft. Just glad it didn't hit the rotors and kill the crew."

"Yeah, no shit," I say. "That had to be scary."

"Clipped the FLIR pod right off the bottom." Officer Coates whistles. "Heard whatever it was really hauled ass. Probably just a near miss collision."

I nod. "Yeah. Probably. Hey, speaking of stuff that got past the ward..." I tell them about the cockatrice walking onto the bus this morning.

"Screw that," says Coates. "Ain't going anywhere near one of those things."

"First that flyby, now a cockatrice?" Brinneman whistles. "Things are going to get interesting."

"There's gotta be a breach in the ward somewhere. Oh, you guys are up." I point at the clerk staring expectantly at the cops.

"Something's brewing... and it's gonna suck," mutters Coates.

You guys have no idea.

When my turn at the register comes, I smile and hand the guy the list... and about twenty minutes later, I'm out the door carrying a double stacked tray with two more floating in front of me. Judging by the reaction of the guys when I return to the station, I'm a conquering hero back from a long-waged campaign of victory. Lieutenant Sims comes out of the back hall to collect his cup—and Lawrence is right behind him.

Oh boy. Here we go.

"Another weird one?" I ask.

Lawrence nods. "Another spontaneous combustion."

"That qualifies as weird." I offer a sheepish smile. "No idea you were coming or I'd have got you something from Starbucks."

"It's fine. I've already had three cups."

I blink. "It's not even seven yet."

"I know." He chuckles. "Hoping you might see something here that didn't exist at the last scene."

Sims gives us a nod.

Lawrence heads for the garage door. I follow him out to the SUV, climb in, and take a long swig from my caramel latte.

"What happened here?"

"Single male victim went up in his recliner. Robert Winslow, age seventy-seven. Lived alone. Time of death is a little fuzzy at the moment. The ME hasn't finished examining the feet."

"Feet?" I stop with my lips a half-inch from the cup. "That sounds gruesome."

"It's not unheard of in a lot of these supposed cases of spontaneous human combustion. Sometimes the feet and hands survive the burn. According to that 'wick theory,' there's not enough fat there to sustain the fire. In this case, the hands were gone, but both feet and about six inches of leg remained... still wearing his slippers."

"Gah. Great, now I'm seeing that in my mind."

Lawrence gives me the side eye. "Getting a vision from here?"

"No, just imagination. I'm picturing old man feet still in their slippers."

He chuckles. "I don't need much imagination to see that every night."

"Aww, you're not old."

"I appreciate the sentiment, young lady, but I'm not afraid of the truth."

"Fifty-two isn't old. Eighty is old." I sip coffee. "Or 2,800 and change."

"Oh, don't be ridiculous." Lawrence laughs.

I lean toward him and flash the big eyes. "My dad's somewhere around that age."

Much to my surprise, he doesn't flinch. "Yeah, but I ain't one of them... whatever you called it. You might not consider fifty-two old for a person, but it's ridiculous for a dog. That 2800 nonsense don't mean a damn thing to me." He smiles. "But thank you for trying to make me feel better."

"No problem. Guess there's no obvious signs of anyone wanting to hurt this guy?"

"Not a one. He did, however, like his whiskey. Found a tumbler glass on the table next to the chair as well as a bottle."

"Is that significant? I mean, beyond you mentioning last time that victims of this are usually alcoholics?"

He offers a noncommittal shrug. "Well, the booze didn't catch fire or appear involved as an accelerant if that's what you're asking. If he was severely inebriated at the time of the fire, it might've prevented him from putting himself out."

"If this is the same situation as the Perez fire, he would've died before any sign of flame appeared to the outside world... except maybe smoke coming out of his nose."

He nods.

A short ride later, we pull up to a row house in Fairhill on Mutter Street. It's a cramped one-way that nearly forces Lawrence to put the drivers' side wheels up on the sidewalk to get past a few larger parked vehicles. He heads around the corner past the end of the block to park, and we walk a ways back to the site of the fire.

The same horrible smell from the Perez house hits me as soon as we're inside. Black smudges cover the ceiling above a recliner that's surprisingly intact. It's got a scorch mark in the general shape of a body—with a generous rear end—on it, but unlike the bed at the last place, the chair could probably be repaired. Most of the damage appears confined to the upholstery. The feet (of the victim) are nowhere in sight, most likely at the ME's office.

A three-quarters-gone bottle of Jack Daniels sits on a tiny wooden end table next to the recliner, no sign of damage to the table or anything else. It's almost like a death ray from space took out the dude and left everything else intact. Only, that probably would've left a hole in the ceiling.

"TV was on when the police showed up," says Lawrence.

"Who called it in?" I walk around the chair, studying it. Sure looks like the guy just went foom where he sat.

"A guy from a service that delivers food to elderly residents who live alone." He looks over his notepad. "Juan Ortiz, from New Leaf. Came by with Mr. Winslow's breakfast, found the scene you're looking at now... only with the feet still standing in front of the chair. They didn't even fall over."

I cringe. "At least the guy was nice enough to leave a drink out for whoever had to deal with that sight."

Lawrence grimaces.

"Okay, here goes." Maybe I can get lucky and avoid touching greasy ashes this time.

I sit on the floor next to the chair in case something in the vision makes me collapse, then grab the armrest and concentrate on wanting to *see*. Usually, violent or traumatic death leaves a fairly strong 'psychic recording' in an object involved with the death or touching the victim. While I do feel an imprint in the chair, it's not as strong as I'd expect. A bit of mental prodding at it peels it open and my vision shifts.

Once again, I'm floating near the ceiling, gazing down at the same room I'm already in. Most of the light comes from a nice-sized TV, but it's tuned into some political commentary show where a bunch of guys in fancy suits complain about other people and policies. Well, that explains why Winslow didn't wake up. This is some weapons-grade boredom. A small lamp on the same table as the whiskey gives off a feeble amount of light. The bottle has the same amount inside, so the food delivery guy didn't help himself to much if any.

Mr. Winslow's sitting in the chair, head slumped forward in sleep. I wouldn't call the guy fat, but he's not exactly skinny. His white hair, burgundy bathrobe, and posture makes him look like a kindly grandfatherly type. I've barely started to take in the scene when dark smoke puffs from his nostrils with his breaths.

He looks so sweet and harmless, I want to grab and shake him awake to warn him, but it's only a vision and I can't move. His body jerks once, then slumps slightly more. Fire bursts out of his gut, creeping upward as the bathrobe catches. Eventually, his chest caves in revealing a hollowed cavity full of glowing embers.

Reality comes back with little fanfare.

"You get anything?" asks Lawrence.

"Yeah."

"Is it a good sign that you didn't jump?" He offers a hand to help me up.

"Thanks." I let him pull me to my feet. "Looks like the same situation as the Perez fire. Pretty sure he died when an internal fire reached his heart. Still can't tell if he had a massive heart attack from the pain or if physical damage killed him, but I don't think he felt much. Couldn't tell if he'd been drunk."

Lawrence records me describing the vision.

"Other than the guy burning in that chair, I didn't see anything unusual. No one leaning in the window to throw fire at him."

"Kinda bizarre to have two cases of spontaneous human combustion so soon. You think there's a mage somewhere using some kind of delayed immolation type spell?"

I fold my arms, looking around. "I have no idea about magic. Couldn't even tell you if a spell like that even exists. The police have mage detectives who'd be better off looking into who killed him if it really is a deliberate act. I got nothin' here other than he went *foom* while sleeping in that chair."

Lawrence bows his head in defeat. "All right. You hear about that cockatrice got in the city earlier?"

"Hear about it? I saw the damn thing. It walked right onto my bus."

"Oh, you gotta tell me about that."

I head for the hallway deeper into the house. "Yeah, sure. Let me poke around a bit and see if I get any hits from other things. Might be a clue in here somewhere."

"All right."

AN HOUR AND TWENTY MINUTES OF USELESSNESS COMES TO AN END with Lawrence driving me back to the station house. Mr. Winslow must have been a sedate guy. I didn't pick up a single psychic imprint on anything else in that place.

Once I'm at the station, I sneak out to the shady spot behind the building to call Mom. She's fine, and still thinks I'm being paranoid about nonsense. Part of me almost wishes they'd hurry up and do something so I can stop living in constant worry. It's exhausting.

Nine minutes into the conversation, the alarm goes off.

"Gotta go, Mom. Call."

"Okay, hon. Be careful."

I run inside to get suited up.

---

WE ROLL UP ON A TRAFFIC ACCIDENT INVOLVING A HONDA CIVIC, a vacuum truck full of literal shit, a Silverado, and a cement mixer. Wow. Talk about a clusterfuck.

The Civic has become a hood ornament on the poop transport, which appeared to be halfway through a turn. The pickup hit the pumper truck at the right rear corner probably the same time the cement mixer T-boned the shitmobile, knocking it over sideways on top of the pickup and causing a tank rupture that saturated the two people inside the Chevy in drained septic tank muck. I *thought* I was having a bad day, but I'm doing better than the young couple trapped in the pickup chest-deep in pure horror.

Brown sludge spills out the windows and gloops down to the road, basically going everywhere. The man who'd been driving the pickup appears to have passed out from the stench. Or maybe he whacked his head. I *think* he has blood on his face—it's hard to tell. The woman's still screaming between bouts of throwing up. That they haven't gotten out of the truck tells me they're pinned, or at least the doors are too damaged to open. Yeah, from the look of the Silverado's front end, the poop truck falling on top of it warped the frame. Those doors are stuck... and dripping with ack.

Guess who also gets covered in it.

And you know what really stinks? Poop plus gasoline.

"Jaws," shouts Herlihy.

"Forget them," I yell back. "No time. This mess could go up in flames any second."

Holding my breath, I tromp over, grab the handle and yank, but the damn thing tears off in my grip. The doors are warped from the crush and quite stuck. At least the pour of shit coming in the broken windshield has slowed to a trickle. I throw the broken handle aside and grab the door itself, yanking with both hands hard enough to bend the metal. The second it opens—causing the liquid contents of the cabin to splash down to the road around my boots—the Civic bursts into flames. Sims starts shouting about getting hoses up front... and there's no water to spare at the moment to push the brown sludge into the nearest storm drain.

At least with the slime flowing out from inside the Silverado, I can see the dashboard hasn't collapsed down to pin their legs. The man's bleeding from the nose. Clumps of half-decomposed toilet paper cling to everything... and I think that's a condom hanging on the rearview mirror.

Ugh. This is almost enough to make a demon lose their lunch.

Or their magically-altered s'mores egg and sausage.

Looks like the driver kissed the steering wheel on impact due to not wearing his belt. Either that or the airbag knocked him clean out. Damn, what a shit show—pun intended. This guy had to be going too fast, bet the cement mixer was also going a little fast... and the idiot in the Civic probably cut off the poop truck. Wouldn't be surprised if it had NJ plates. O'Keefe, mistaking me for a girl of ordinary strength, hurries over and helps me pull the guy out while Lancaster struggles at the door on the woman's side, unable to move it.

A cop jogging by on the sidewalk tries to jump across the slime flow, but slips and goes sliding in it. O'Keefe shudders, on the verge of throwing up. We drag the unconscious man out of the truck, the woman scrambling after us under her own power. Lancaster runs around the back end of the wreck, slipping and sliding, and hurries over to help support her. O'Keefe and I drag the man out to a safe distance. That poor woman looks like someone made a statue out of brown clay. She'd been trapped up to her neck in it for however long it took us to get here.

S'mores does a backflip in my gut.

I back up and let the EMTs in, and try not to think about what I'm covered in.

At a guess, I'm going to say the Civic driver didn't make it... the car was small to begin with, but it'd fit in a glove compartment now. Though, I don't see a body inside. All around me, the guys curse and swear at the foulness. The woman from the pickup complains of soreness in her neck, but doesn't appear to have suffered significant injury. She does, however, strip to her underwear right there on the street before asking one of us to turn a hose on her.

Herlihy obliges.

While he's spraying her down, I have a 'screw it' moment and walk over to stand next to her so he can rinse off my coat, pants, and boots.

Sims sends O'Keefe and Lancaster into the spray as well.

No sense getting shit all over the inside of the truck. And yeah, we'll probably be riding home standing on the back ledge.

Did I mention it's in my hair?

WHEN WE RETURN TO THE STATION, I RE-ENACT THAT SCENE FROM THE movie with the space soldiers and the giant bugs: co-ed shower. At the guys' initial surprised looks of me strolling past them naked, I mutter, "Not waiting, and I'm not gonna ask anyone to wait for me. That was fucking nasty."

The guys are total gentlemen about it as far as I can tell, since I'm not really looking at anything but myself and the wonderful bar of soap. Everyone's quiet for a few minutes until O'Keefe grumbles about that being the most disgusting thing he's ever seen.

"They're going to be pumping those people so full of antibiotics they won't catch so much as a cold for the next fifteen years," says Lancaster in the stall next to mine.

Everyone shudders.

"I had a feeling today would suck when a cockatrice walked onto my bus this morning... but I didn't exactly expect two thousand pounds of uncontained sewage."

Herlihy gags.

"Did you see the look on that cop when he got back up," asks Baker, near to laughing.

"About the same look Amari had on her face when she opened that door." Lancaster retches.

Baker's laughter stops. "Oh. Right."

Lamar walks into the stall on my right. "Let he who is not covered in shit cast the first glop."

"That's just nasty," says McCafferty.

"Hey, did the Honda guy make it?" Humberto slams a locker door somewhere off to the left.

Warm wonderful water on my face pushes the memories out of my brain.

"Barely." McCafferty whistles. "First rule of driving a tiny car: do not cut off giant trucks and slam on your brakes. It would be easier to list the bones he *didn't* break."

I let my head sag forward until it touches the wall, hot water cascading down my back. I don't care that I'm the only woman in a room full of guys and most of us are nude. I don't care that I should've been home an hour ago. I don't much care to do anything for the foreseeable future but stand here cocooned in soap and steam, trying to scrub the memory of the last call out of my brain.

"Gonna be smelling that for weeks," grumbles Lancaster.

"Hey, Keefe, you got some TP in your hair," says Humberto.

I throw up a little in the back of my throat.

"I can still smell it," mutters Lancaster.

"Dude, it's all in your head." Herlihy laughs.

Stretching, I turn my back to the spray, which gives me a view of a room full of firemen showering. Evidently, we all have the same idea: stand in the shower until skin falls off. Since none of them are checking me out, I keep my gaze on the floor at my feet. This is totally like one of those things that happens in the Army or something where the whole platoon sees something so damn awful they all agree it never happened.

Yeah... this has been the 'Monday' from hell. Hello, Universe? If you could go ahead and *not* send me any more overturned shit trucks, that would be great. Thanks.

# 12

## THE DELETE BUTTON

An inordinate amount of air-fresheners crops up in the station house Wednesday.

Lieutenant Sims gives me an odd look that I think means he knows we broke the unwritten 'shower protocol.' It's basically an 'I understand, but don't make a habit of it' sort of expression. I nod and carry on with hose inspection... and not the one in the shower. Actual hoses.

It hits me how odd it is that I've never felt the least bit tempted to cheat. Granted, it's impossible to cheat on a guy when I don't have an official boyfriend. But, I consider Jason official, and even in a room full of naked firefighters I didn't at all feel the temptation. Odd that my weak impulse control should not apply in that situation. Maybe it's because I grew up with Mom being so weird about Dad. For most of my life, I assumed myself a child of rape and hated/feared some despicable, faceless male figure who did something so awful to my mother that she couldn't even talk about him. Never in my wildest dreams could I have imagined she suffered a mind-control enchant from an Elestari and seduced Dad.

Though, I'm sure he didn't exactly require much convincing.

The day is slow. A little after one that afternoon, I conspire with

Herlihy to play with Sims' head a little by perching at the opening for the pole on the second story. As soon as the lieutenant walks into the garage area, Herlihy jogs over to the pole, says something about having a fey ancestor, and I pull him upward with telekinesis so it looks like he just slid *up* the pole to the second floor.

That Brian is this huge Viking-looking ginger-bearded dude makes it all the funnier.

Our co-conspirator, Lamar, is hopefully in position to get a good picture of Sims' face.

Yeah. We're bored.

But bored is good... it means no one is burning.

JASON PICKS ME UP AT 6:22 P.M.

I filled in the time between my end-of-shift at six and his arrival on the phone with Mom. She's okay and I'm starting to think that the warmongers might have only talked about kidnapping her as a trick. Just something to drive me crazy without any real intent to do anything to Mom.

"You look beautiful... but tired," says Jason as I climb into his pickup. "Still up for this?"

"Yeah. I need it." I pull the door closed, let my head fall back against the seat, and sigh. "Sorry if I'm a little weary at the moment."

He pulls out onto the street, heading for my place. "Not a problem. Heard you guys had a shitty day."

I groan.

"Couldn't resist."

"Neither can anyone else." I chuckle. "It was so bad no one even noticed I ripped the truck open with my bare hands. I think they all just wanted to get the hell away from that mess as fast as possible."

"Don't blame them. How's your mom?"

"Fine." I spend a few minutes talking about how I've started wondering if it's just a head game. "I mean it makes no sense for them to do it at all, so maybe they're just playing with me."

"What for?"

"Couple hundred years of mind games could make me snap. Maybe I've been thinking about this all wrong. They're not planning anything on the scale of a human lifetime here."

Jason thinks that over for a moment while hunting for a parking space near my building. "That's hard to wrap my brain around."

"Does it bother you that I'm going to live that long?"

He kills the engine and grins at me. "Only in the sense of being somewhat jealous that some other guy will get to spend time with you after I'm gone. Though, I'll eventually be the creepy old guy lucky enough to have a young lady on his arm."

I laugh. "And on that note… be right back."

He nods.

My closet contains one Little Black Dress ™. I decide to let it out to play. For a moment, I consider front-loading another less expensive-slash-delicate thing to wear for hanging out at Jason's place later into the amulet, but nah. I think we've gotten to the point where it wouldn't be weird to be casually naked around him. Of course, if that turns out to be awkward, there's the illusionary outfit or I can steal one of his shirts. Since our plans tonight involve a dark theater and a restaurant, I shimmy into the dress sans underwear… you know, just in case I need to use the tail.

The amulet Natalie made for me hangs out in the open over the plunging neckline, but despite being a little chibi succubus, it doesn't look too out of place. Wonder what she made it out of? Some manner of red enamel with gold outline. I hope she didn't use up too much expensive stuff for me.

Frilly goth stuff aside, I've never been all that into overly femme clothes, but I do have one pair of high heels, shiny black ones, that have ribbon ties instead of straps. I thought them cute—and ridiculously expensive. They're one of the last things I ever stole, a few days before I turned eighteen, and they still look newish because I've only worn them like four times. Honestly, I stole them purely out of protest that someone seriously thought anyone would pay that much for shoes. Kind of a F-U to the nose-in-the-sky crowd. Who pays $2,400 for $38 worth of leather because some French dude puts his name on something?

And okay, maybe I stole them because I *couldn't* afford them.

I hit the perfume a little heavier than normal out of paranoia that some lingering reek from the septic truck may remain somewhere that I can't detect since my brain decided it's no longer on speaking terms with my nose... at least for a few more days.

Once dressed, I hurry back down to the truck. Jason spends a moment or two staring at me.

"Yeah, I know. I'm impersonating a female at the moment."

He chuckles. "You're astoundingly beautiful."

"Why thank you, Mr. Dunn." I fake fan myself.

He drives to his place and runs inside to change out of his uniform to a nice dark blue-grey shirt and black pants. From there, we head downtown to a nice but not over-the-top Italian restaurant. I try to pick something I'll be able to finish, so I order this clams-and-mussels over pasta dish. He tries the lobster ravioli.

Our attempt at normal conversation over dinner starts off with fire department stuff, though I avoid talking about the accident since I'm trying to eat. It soon drifts into matters of a more esoteric nature when he asks about Mom. For some reason, I decide to just open up and whine at him about how annoyed I am that the 'forces of evil' are threatening my mother and how it makes no sense, and how I only want to be left out of the whole destroying the world thing. He listens patiently until I catch myself feeling too much like a kid who wants someone else to make the bad stuff stop happening.

"That's a bit of a mess, yeah." He takes a sip of wine. "You're right though. Even the idiots who want to go back to killing each other ought to be able to figure out it's stupid to threaten someone who'll die anyway if you blow up the Earth." He gets a strange grin for a few seconds, but forces it away. "What if you try and act blasé, like it wouldn't bother you?"

"Jason, that's my mother."

"Right. Hence, *act*. If they think you wouldn't care, they'd leave her alone."

I stab a mussel with my fork. "Yeah but I couldn't be like that in front of her. What if *she* didn't realize I was bluffing?"

"I'm sure she'd understand."

"She still doesn't believe any of this is real."

He rushes a mouthful of food. "Didn't you show her the wings?"

"Yeah." I twirl linguini around the mussel. "I can't tell if she's just trying to not think about it or if she's really having a mental thing and refusing to let it in. Maybe the shock of it went beyond her ability to process and she just ignored it."

Jason quirks an eyebrow. "Can't you peek into people's thoughts?"

"That's my mother!" I gasp, then wind up snickering. "I mean, I realize I grew up in a trailer park, but I'm pretty sure mind-reading my own mother is taboo."

He sputters, nearly choking on laughter.

Our conversation continues on a lighter tone from there, mostly about the musical we're going to see, *Cats*, being older than hell and still on stage. Hell, I'll probably still be able to catch a show of it 300 years from now... assuming the world still exists.

---

I'VE FOUND A NEW AWESOME HOBBY WHILE SITTING IN THE DARK theater next to Jason.

Every so often, I use my telekinesis to move random small objects on the stage to mess with the actors. Gotta give 'em credit though. None have broken character or flubbed a line—though they've made some interesting faces.

Though I shouldn't call it a *new* hobby. Doing it at a professional theater production is the new part. I've been using telekinesis as an outlet for restless energy most of my life. Moving teachers' chairs out from under them when they go to sit down, disappearing dry erase markers or light wands... Probably the worst thing I ever did with TK was when I de-pantsed this kid Patrick during the fifth grade talent show. He used to pick on me mercilessly for being poor, so while he was in the middle of singing—make that murdering—*Sweet Child o'*

*Mine,* I gave the entire school a look at his cartoon briefs. Thinking back on it, I kinda regret doing it. He went from extrovert to introvert overnight. But at least he never picked on me again.

Anyway... cats.

I lean against Jason and enjoy the rest of the show.

---

AFTER THE THEATER, WE HEAD TO JASON'S PLACE.

I leave my shoes by the door, happy to be free from heels, and join him on the sofa. He's not big on drinking due to his father being a mean alcoholic, so we sip iced green tea while unwinding and talking about the show.

"I liked it, but they kinda overacted a little," says Jason.

"How so?"

He waves about as if trying to grab a word out of the air. "Not sure how to explain it. They kept making these strange bug-eyed expressions that didn't seem to fit what was going on at the time."

I die laughing.

Jason gives me the side eye. "I sense some foul play was afoot."

"A little." I make a pinchy gesture. "Some random little items might've been moving around the stage on their own."

He cackles, then sets his tea down, rolls toward me, and attacks with tickling fingers. "Sounds like someone needs to be punished."

I squeal and squirm away while laughing, trying not to spill my drink. The next thing I know, I'm draped across his lap and he's patting my ass. I prop my chin up on one hand, tapping a finger at my cheek.

"You know, I don't think I've ever been spanked. Is that where you're going?"

He hums appraisingly while rubbing my rear end. "Not sure. You just kinda wound up there."

"We could try it if you want, but I'm not at all into cuffs or being tied up or anything like that."

Jason's hands keep roaming around my body. "That's good since I don't have any. Not really into that sort of thing either. Though, it is kinda ironic."

"What's ironic?"

"Your being a half... *not*-demon and having no temptation to get kinky. Figured the demons would be all about that stuff."

"Oh, it's usually the prim and proper types who are. I bet the Elestari have some super twisted sex." I roll over and smile up at him. "Blame the cops. I hate being confined."

"Seems like it would be pretty difficult to contain you." He leans down and kisses me.

"If I knew then what I know now..." I kiss him back. "I'd probably be in a cage somewhere in a secret government facility."

His eyebrows go up. "That bad?"

"Well, cops hate it when people break out of jail. Especially if the 'break' part is literal."

"You never told me you did time."

I giggle. "Because I really didn't. Longest I ever spent locked up was a weekend. They detained me a lot, but I never really got charged with anything. Call it 'taxpayer-funded babysitting.' You know, now that I think about it, maybe I was using mental influence on the cops without even realizing it."

"You've definitely charmed me." He grins.

"Jason?" I reach up and grab his shirt, pulling him down until our noses touch. "I think we should go upstairs before we wind up on the floor again."

He scoops me up and stands. "Your wish is my command."

———

IT'S GOTTA BE AFTER ONE IN THE MORNING BY THE TIME WE STOP.

Messing with actors isn't the most fun I've ever had with telekinesis. It can certainly make for some interesting positions. Whoever wrote the *Kama Sutra* couldn't even have imagined the effect levitation has on lovemaking. Jason's splayed out on the bed like he'd fallen out of an airplane, staring at the ceiling with a dumbfounded grin. Hmm. Maybe I am a succubus after all. He does kind of look like I drained his life energy out via his groin.

I roll toward him, sliding one arm and one leg across him. My chibi succubus amulet dangles down to his chest. He shifts his eyes to meet mine.

"You can't possibly be ready for round... three?"

I tap a fingertip to his nose. "You mean five?"

He emits a nervous laugh.

"No... just want to cuddle. I'm tired."

Jason smiles. "Sorry for keeping you up too late. The morning's going to be rough."

"Thank you for a wonderful night." I let my head rest on his shoulder, wondering if it's a bad sign that his skin feels warm to me. Then again, an ice cube would feel warm compared to dry ice. "Tonight was like a delete button for the awful 'Monday' I had yesterday."

"I suppose disgusting traffic accidents and stray cockatrices are better than chasing a serial arsonist. Speaking of... how's Lawrence doing?"

"He's better. Back on duty already."

"Ahh, cool." Jason starts stroking my hair. Mmm. That's nice. "What's he up to?"

"Oh, the usual... trying to figure out why old people are spontaneously combusting."

# 13

## GOOD TIMING

Somehow, I manage to wake up Thursday morning when Jason's alarm goes off.

We shower together, which is more annoying than I thought it would be for two reasons: we don't have time to fool around, and I can't run only the hot water with a normal human under the spray. Still, what little playfulness occurs while we wash each other's hard-to-reach places is nice.

He about faints when I walk outside naked, carrying my dress, bag, and heels.

By the time he's at the door, my illusory clothing is on. He blinks, staring at me with an expression of utter confusion.

"Did you..."

I grin. "I did."

"How'd you get dressed so fast?"

"Easy. I didn't." I tap the amulet. "It's an illusion. Gotta run home to get my uniform... and we're going to two different stations, so..."

"You want cereal or eggs or something?" He points back over his shoulder with a thumb.

"Thanks, but, no time."

He hurries over to give me a goodbye-for-now kiss. "Stay safe."

"That goes for you more." I poke him in the stomach. "I've got armor."

Jason salutes me. "Yes, ma'am."

I pat him on the cheek, concentrate on the 'don't notice me' mental thing, and pop my wings. Natalie would totally squeal at me flying around in the illusionary outfit she designed. I do look like the 'doom faerie' she called me, only larger.

On the flight back to my apartment, I think about all the times the cops picked me up as a kid and how a few of them should've ended with me landing in front of a juvenile court judge and probably time in a correctional facility. I had to have been using mental influence on the cops to go easy on me. That time we stole a car should've been a couple months detention, but they treated me like I'd only violated curfew.

Hmm. I wonder if I can do that mental influence thing on purpose? What nursing school was it Tracy said she attended? Gotta look that up.

TODAY, I ANNOUNCE THE STARBUCKS RUN WHILE STROLLING INTO THE station.

Okay, that's not unusual. I'm usually the one who initiates it. What is unusual is my ordering a large redeye plus a triple espresso. No sooner do I pick up the order at the counter than the alarm goes off at the station house. It's loud enough to hear from inside the Starbucks.

Shit.

There are a few ways to get a room full of people to stare at you. One of them is chugging a scalding-hot venti redeye that just came out of the machine.

"Fire call. Didn't want it to get cold. Thanks."

Leaving everyone to their stunned silence, I run out carrying twelve other cups in trays, my triple-espresso floating along beside me. The guys are jumping on the truck as I careen in the door. I drop the coffee on the table at the side of the garage and race to my locker to get my gear. Since they're ready to roll out already, I just carry my stuff with me into the truck and put it on as we drive.

We roll to a stop in Whitman, in front of a row house on Roseberry Street. There's already a small crowd gathered on the sidewalk around an African American couple not much older than me. Of everyone here, they're freaking out the most, so I'm guessing the fire's in their house.

A thin trail of smoke rises into the air from behind the buildings. There's no easy way into the backyards of these places, so it's in the front door. I grab the first hose and take point, rushing toward a small inferno in the kitchen. While the fire has only started to creep into the hallway, the kitchen ceiling is almost gone. Outside, Herlihy yells questions about if anyone else is in the house and I catch the woman saying something about a cat.

For the moment, it appears that the burn hasn't gotten too far out of the kitchen, so I'm not *too* worried about kitty. I yank open the valve and throw water at the orange stuff. O'Keefe and Lancaster bring in a second hose a moment after me. Boards fall in from the ceiling, giving us a view of the upstairs bathroom. The window over the sink has already broken out, so I don't think we need to cut any new holes in the wall for ventilation. We make relatively short work of the fire... this kitchen isn't that big.

One stubborn lump of unidentifiable crap on the floor keeps burning. I hose it again, but the water pressure cuts the blob into several smaller patches of fire.

"Shit!" I yell. "Got a grease ball in here. Someone grab a Class B."

While O'Keefe makes exploratory holes in the walls to check for embers, I telekinetically gather the bits of smoldering black grease together in the middle of the room. Though... it didn't explode or flare under water, so maybe it's not oil. Still, it's continuing to burn despite being doused.

Lamar arrives with a dry extinguisher and hoses the burning lump. And still, it doesn't go out. He keeps spraying it for a full two minutes before all signs of combustion finally disappear.

"Don't think that's grease," says O'Keefe.

Lamar nods.

"Yeah…" I stare suspiciously at the black patch of floor, no longer a lump. "Whatever it was, it just kept on burning until it consumed itself." I don't want to say out loud that the original lump was about the same size as a curled-up cat. In fact, I kinda hate that I even thought that.

Maybe I've been spending too much time with Lawrence playing 'arson investigator,' but I can't help myself. Once we're done checking the downstairs and inspecting upstairs for any further sign of fire, I head outside and approach the young couple who lives here.

Both lean back with surprised expressions when I remove my breathing mask. Guess they weren't expecting a woman. Or maybe it's my paper-white face…

"This your house?" I ask.

They nod.

"Brooklyn Amari with the Philadelphia Fire Department." I offer a hand.

"Dashawn Foster," says the man while shaking my hand. "This is my wife, Lanette."

"Did you find Jinx?" asks Lanette.

"Your cat?"

She nods.

"Umm. I don't think so." I bite my lip. At least I really hope I didn't. "Do you know how the fire started?"

"Not really," says Dashawn. "I was lugging some laundry upstairs, Lanette's downstairs swearin' at the Xbox, and—"

She swats him on the arm.

"Well, you was, woman." He catches her fist and pulls her into a hug. "Girl gets kinda upset at the games. Anyway, I'm halfway up the stairs when *boom!* There's this giant-ass explosion, shook the whole damn house. Laundry basket goes flyin'. I run back down stairs and the whole damn kitchen is a fireball."

"We ran outside." Lanette looks around nervously. "He called 911 on his cell since he had it on him. You really didn't see our Jinx?"

"Nope." I turn toward the other firefighters still wandering in and out of the house. "Anyone seen a cat?"

Negative replies come from everyone.

"She's probably hiding in the house somewhere. Or went out a window." Dashawn eyes a smallish tree two houses to the left. "Been a while since I had to get a cat out of a tree."

Humberto pats him on the back. "What'd you do, grab the trunk and shake?"

I can't help but laugh. Brian Herlihy is like six foot and change and probably past three hundred pounds, with a fluffy ginger beard.

He starts to laugh, but fake scowls. "Careful I don't grind your bones into bread."

"Huh?" Humberto tilts his head.

"Ay, didn't your mother read to you when you were little?" I ask in Spanish before switching to English. "You called him a giant, and he's rolling with it."

Humberto grins but gives us both the finger and resumes gathering hose.

"Jinx!" shouts Lanette. "Jinxie?"

Ugh. I really hope that greasy lump that wouldn't go out wasn't a case of spontaneous feline combustion. A bad feeling settles in my gut, so I head back inside to the kitchen. It doesn't stink anywhere near as bad as the ash left over from those two bizarre fires, though a smell that reminds me of the other underlying stink saturates the room. Lacking the fetid awfulness of incinerated human covering it, the fragrance is basically fresh mushrooms with a hint of burned zucchini.

I pick at the black patch with my boot, but don't see anything that looks like bone fragments. There's a little hope at least. If I'm not staring at the cat's remains, then the cat must be somewhere. I head to the front of the house, specifically the stairs. With all the commotion of us going in and out, I bet the cat would've gone to the most remote part of the house away from the front door.

Once on the second story, I start calling for Jinx. Upon entering the master bedroom at the front end of the house, I'm rewarded with a growl from under the bed. I've never had a pet before. My mother was pretty much right to assume I lacked the discipline necessary to take care of one at that age. Also, we couldn't have afforded one. Mom barely managed to feed us. Maybe I could swing a cat or hamster or something now. I guess Ashley sorta counts as a pet, right? Even if she came pre-housebroken.

Still, I'm quite relieved to find the cat alive. I crouch down and peer under the bed. An all-black cat with bright teal eyes has crammed itself as far back into the corner as possible. The second it sees me, it goes into this yowling, hissing fit. Okay, maybe kitty's not a fan of extraplanar beings. Suppose there's telekinesis to get the cat out of there, but I can't exactly put my armor on at the moment without making a scene. Making an already freaked-out cat fly around is just asking for blood.

I stand back up and shout down the stairs for someone to send Lanette inside.

The woman hurries in and looks up past the spilled laundry basket at me.

"Found the cat. He's a little upset."

"She," says Lanette, stepping around clothes on her way up. "Oh, thank God she's all right."

Not sure why people always thank 'god' for stuff like this. Like... someone survives a tornado ripping their house in half. Don't they say this god is like all-powerful or something? Given that, who do they think sent the tornado in the first place? Praising some deity for surviving a natural disaster the deity created is about as nonsensical as a person asking the guy who just mugged them for a ride to the hospital.

Lanette crouches down and tries to coax the cat out, but the animal continues yowling and hissing. Wow, okay... maybe it's *not* freaking out at me for being a little extra.

"Aww, sweetie, come on out," coos Lanette. "What's wrong, baby?"

"Probably panicking over the fire." I take a knee and look at the cat again. Hmm. I wonder if my mental powers work on animals?

Focused on thoughts of 'Kitty, calm thy shit,' I stare into the cat's eyes...

And the bedroom swirls into a blur. The fog clears a second later and I'm standing in the unburned kitchen, looking at Jinx pawing at an empty food dish. She crosses the room and leaps up onto the counter, approaching a large wooden bowl full of fresh vegetables. The cat meows a few times loud, as if trying to yell at someone to come feed her. Video game sounds and a woman's voice calling something a cheating piece of shit come from the hallway. Back and forth, the cat walks, rubbing up against the bowl. The fifth time she brushes against it, the bowl slides off the counter, tumbles over—and detonates on impact with the floor.

A bloom of orange-red flames rises in a column that touches the ceiling, spreading out in a carpet of flames all the way to the walls. Jinx shrieks and leaps off the counter, narrowly missing a rain of embers. Shouts, and the thuds of Mr. Foster falling down the stairs come from the front of the house.

I snap back to the here and now, stare still locked with the cat.

She stops growling and gazes deep into my soul.

Hmm. I'm not getting any read of intention like I do with people, but it seems like I've successfully hit Jinx over the head with the mellow-hammer. A little telekinetic tug drags her within arms' reach. I scoop her up and stand, petting her.

"Now she looks stoned," says Lanette.

"My fault. I'm a little bit psychic and I tried to calm her down."

"Oh. That's cool." She reaches for the cat, which I hand over. "Hey, if you're psychic, can you figure out how the fire started?"

I chuckle.

She raises both eyebrows. "I ain't tryin' ta be funny."

"Oh, I know. I'm chuckling because I already have."

"No shit."

"Yep." I pat Jinx on the head. "Your cat started it, but not intentionally."

She looks at me like I said the dumbest thing in the world. "You think a cat would start a fire on purpose?"

"Mystral Cats would if someone pissed them off enough."

"Yeah, but they ain't allowed in the city." She squeezes Jinx tight to her chest and smooches his head a few times. "How'd *my* cat set off a fire?"

"You had a bowl of veggies on the kitchen counter. Cat knocked them off and they exploded when they hit the floor."

Lanette stares at me. Apparently 'I'm psychic' is cool, but 'your vegetables exploded' has crossed the line.

"I found a burning lump that wouldn't go out. Pretty sure that lump was what remained of the vegetables. If I had to guess, I'd say they had a dangerous enchantment on them."

"Oh. Umm..." She stops looking at me like I've gone crazy. "Why would anyone do that?"

"That's a good question. You didn't eat any of them yet did—" My turn to blink and stare into space. Holy shit. Those spontaneous combustion cases... both times I saw the fire starting in the stomach area. Lawrence told me about that wick effect thing and I assumed it would've gone to the gut for abdominal fat, but... what if the fire *started* there. "Umm. Where did you get those vegetables?"

Lanette scratches her head. "At the corner market couple blocks over. And no, I just got 'em yesterday on the way home from work. Didn't eat any of it yet."

"Good. Yeah, the cat might've charred your kitchen, but she saved your lives." I guide her to the door. "C'mon outside until the fire marshal clears the place."

Content to cling to her cat, she goes back outside to stand by Dashawn.

I head over to the truck and dig my phone out from under my fire retardant leggings.

"What's up?" asks Lieutenant Sims, walking over.

"Oh, hey LT. Kitchen fire, but it didn't come from cooking." I dial Lawrence. "I think I got a break on those other two fires."

"Same thing?"

"Well, not exactly. No one died here... though a cat probably shit its proverbial pants."

"Hello?" asks Lawrence from the phone.

I hit speaker and lean closer to Sims. "Hey. It's Amari..." I proceed to explain about the detonating vegetables, the greasy lump, and the familiar 'earthy/mushroom' scent that I also caught a whiff of at the spontaneous combustion sites. It makes sense to me now as the after-smell of self-immolating veggies. "The visions I got at both other fires showed the fire starting in their stomachs. I'm thinking they ate something like these veggies that ignited while they slept."

Sims whistles. "Wow... so what are we dealing with here? Serial arsonist or a nut-job doing it randomly?"

"Could be," says Lawrence. "You get anything on where the vegetables are coming from?"

"The resident said they bought them at a corner market not far from here. I was going to go check it out if it's okay with the lieutenant."

"Once we're done here, go for it." Sims nods.

"Want me to head out that way?" asks Lawrence.

"I don't think it's really necessary to bother you with it, but if you want to... I'll wait."

"Nah, go ahead. Give me a call if you need more official authority." Lawrence chuckles.

"All right. Thanks." I hang up, pocket my phone, and head back into the fray to help clear the scene.

---

EVENTUALLY, THE FIRE MARSHAL DECLARES THE BURN OFFICIALLY OUT and gives the Fosters the all clear to go back inside so they can grab clothes or whatever they need to take with them to wherever they are going to stay. I stash my hat, coat, and fire-resistant leggings in the truck.

"Amari?" asks Herlihy when I close the door without getting in. "Sticking around?"

"Following up on some investigative stuff. Go enjoy that cold Starbucks."

The guys laugh.

After assuring them I can get back to the station, I head off on foot following the directions Lanette gave me. A couple blocks over and three up, a small non-chain convenience store sits on the corner with a sizeable produce display outside. Basically, a bunch of milk crates and tables set up with boxes of various fruits and vegetables. I pick up random cucumbers, lettuce heads, tomatoes and such, but none of them give off any odd energy or contain any psychic imprints.

Soon after I start poking around the boxes, a short friendly-looking guy with brown skin emerges from the store. His white apron has some serious stains, but none appear to be blood.

"Need help finding anything?" he asks in English with a thick accent.

"Maybe," I reply in Spanish. "I'm Brooklyn Amari with the fire department. We're investigating a potential arson case."

"Javier Vasquez," replies the man, offering a handshake. "You think my little store has something to do with it?"

"Not directly. Yesterday, do you remember a woman buying vegetables here? Mid-twenties, black. Probably showed up after 5 p.m.?"

He shrugs. "Lot of people buy stuff here. I don't remember them all."

"Lanette Foster?"

"Oh. Yeah. She comes here a couple times a week." Javier nods. "Bought some peppers, tomatoes, onions."

I pluck a big green pepper from a nearby box and study it, though it appears normal in every way. It's tempting to drop it to see if it explodes, but I don't think it will... and the store owner probably wouldn't appreciate it.

"Where do you get these from? Have you noticed anyone tampering with the stock?"

He scratches at his chest. "All over. I get from a bunch of local growers, farmers' markets and stuff. That's why people come here. I save them from having to drive so far. All fresh and local. Tampering? No... why?"

"We believe someone is magically tampering with produce and causing it to become incendiary."

"There hasn't been anyone messing around with my stock." He points up at a small camera. "Always keeping an eye on it."

"Do you have any idea where the particular veggies that Lanette bought came from?"

"Umm." He shrugs. "Do you have the receipt?"

"No... fair bet it burned."

"Oh." He goes wide-eyed. "Is she all right?"

I nod. "Yeah. They got lucky. Cat knocked the bowl of produce off the counter before they ate it."

Javier cringes. "Glad they're okay. I can give you a list, but there's a lot of different places I buy from."

"Okay... thanks."

"No problem. Sure you don't need anything?"

"Thanks, but I'm still on duty. Gotta shop on my own time."

He nods.

One final look over the produce fails to reveal any suspicious energy. I wander off to the curb and pull out my phone.

Lawrence picks up after a few rings. "Hey... any luck?"

"Not really. I found the market, but all the vegetables here look normal. Says he gets them from a whole bunch of different places. I'm pretty sure the two unexplained spontaneous combustion cases probably ate some form of magically tainted veggies. Trick is figuring out where they came from. Not much more for me to do here."

"All right. I'll check with the meal service that visited Mr. Winslow. See where they got the food from."

"You said that service showed up for breakfast, right? Who brought him dinner?"

"Right... No idea. Possibly the same service." Lawrence sighs. "Exploding damn carrots. What's next?"

"Ugh. Never ask that..."

# 14

## UNSAFE LEVELS OF SPICINESS

Lawrence wants me to meet him at the Winslow fire site.

After getting that list of farmers' markets from Javier, I duck into an alley for enough privacy to let my wings out. The flight to Fairhill is short and uneventful. Since I'm likely way ahead of Lawrence, I decide to start ringing doorbells. Hey, he didn't say anything about not doing anything until he got here.

A late-fifties white dude answers the door one house to the left in a tank top and grey pants. The same sort of nondescript grey 'old man' pants they must sell at Grandpas R Us. "Dammit, will you people leave me alone already? I ain't got the money to be handing it out to beggars."

"I'm not here to ask you to donate. I'm investigating the fire next door."

"Oh." The guy's hostility ratchets back a few notches. "Not sure what I can help with."

"Did you know Mr. Winslow?"

"Not really. Lived next door to the guy for maybe fifteen years, but didn't see him much. He kept to himself. Stayed inside most of the time. Think he had his son visiting him a couple times a week."

"His son? Or a meal service?"

He shrugs. "Could'a been either. Same dude would come by three times a week."

"No one else visited him? And he never left the house, like to go shopping for food?"

"Nah. At least not that I ever saw. Who knows what he did durin' the day. I ain't retired yet."

I nod. Yeah, this guy is about as helpful as an air conditioner in Alaska. "Understood. Thanks for your help."

"Crazy shit that…" The man huffs. "Is it true the poor bastard just went up in flames out of the blue?"

"So far, it looks like that."

"World gets weirder every day." He backs up a step and closes the door.

Lawrence pulls up in the arson unit SUV as I'm walking past Winslow's place to the other side neighbor. I wait for him at the door, and ring the bell as soon as he's standing next to me.

"You got here quick," says Lawrence.

"Caught a tailwind. Neighbor on the left didn't have anything useful."

"Right…"

"And it looks like no one is home here."

Lawrence checks his phone. "It is the middle of the day. People are likely at work."

"Doubt the neighbors would be much use anyway." Lawrence starts back toward his truck. "I don't believe Mr. Winslow had much social interaction. Up for checking out the food delivery place?"

"Sure why not."

---

TWELVE MINUTES LATER, WE PARK DOWNTOWN IN FRONT OF A SMALL restaurant on the corner called New Leaf. Painted words on the glass indicate the place is all about organic and healthy alternatives. According to Lawrence, this is the place that runs the food delivery to elders.

We head inside and wind up speaking to the day manager, a Rastafarian who introduces himself as Kai. The man also appears to be one of the cooks, as he's wearing a black apron with a bright green 'New Leaf' logo. After a somewhat confusing and ultimately pointless conversation about where he gets his produce from, Lawrence asks about the meal deliveries.

"Oh yeah." Kai nods. "We service a list of maybe a hundred twenty people 'round the area. Doin' this pay-it-forward ting where people who come here ta eat can donate a couple bucks, an' that helps offset the cost o' feedin' the elders. Sometimes, the people, dey get their own stuff and my crew jus' go there an' cook it for dem. Sometimes, mix o' bot'."

"Have any of your customers or meal delivery clients experienced anything unusual?" I ask.

Kai half-shrugs, turning his hands palm up. "Like wot ya mean 'unusual?'"

"Like vegetables exploding or starting fires."

"Some of our dishes are spicy, but not *that* spicy." Kai chuckles. "You serious?"

"Yeah." I'm not picking up on any feelings of worry or guilt from the guy, so I look over the other three employees: two women and a man all about the same thirtysomething age. They, too, don't appear to be involved. "Magic's involved."

"Ahh. Little good will come o' dat," says Kai.

Lawrence pulls out his notepad. "What did you send Mr. Winslow for dinner last Monday?"

"Umm. One sec." Kai walks around behind the counter and checks a computer. "Onsite. My guy went there for C&C."

"C&C?" I ask.

"Cookin' and conversation." Kai smiles. "We show up, cook with whatever's on hand, and spend a while keeping the client company."

"Great." I hang my head. "So whatever blew up was something Winslow already had in his kitchen... but according to that neighbor, he never went out."

"Is Juan Ortiz in today?" asks Lawrence.

"Yeah." Kai nods at us before gesturing at the other guy behind the counter. "Hey, Juan."

The guy looks up, and right away I can tell he's still a bit rattled from finding Mr. Winslow's remains. He approaches with some caution.

"Hi." I introduce myself, then Lawrence. "We're looking into the fire. I understand you prepared his meal the night before you found him?"

"Yeah." Juan fidgets.

He's on edge, but I'm not sensing guilt off him. "What did you prepare for him? Did anything odd happen while you cooked?"

"Ehh... Sautéed some vegetables and chicken. Wasn't a lot to work with there. He had some fresh squash, carrots, potatoes, and an onion in the fridge... and a pack of supermarket chicken in the freezer."

"Any idea where it came from?" Lawrence scribbles in his pad, then looks up.

"He said Betty brought them over to share since she got too many for herself to eat before it all spoiled. And yeah, something kinda weird did happen. I kept smelling burned stuff while cooking, but couldn't figure out where it came from. You think I had maybe a premonition?"

I glance at Lawrence, then back to Juan. "I suppose it's possible. Where does this Betty live?"

"All he said was 'down the street a ways.'"

"We should go check on her." Lawrence flips his pad closed.

"Yeah... that's probably a good idea."

---

LAWRENCE AND I SPLIT UP AND GO HOUSE-TO-HOUSE UP AND DOWN Winslow's street.

I'm seven doors south from the place when Lawrence whistles to get my attention. He's two doors back on the opposite side of the street, beckoning me with a wave, so I trot over.

"What's up?"

"The older couple who lives here knows a Betty Reed. She lives five houses that way. Likes to visit the elders and check up on them."

"I have a bad feeling."

Lawrence starts walking. "Yeah, me too."

We stop at another row house with a little too much mail in the box.

"Oh, dammit." I sigh at the sidewalk before stepping up to the door and ringing the bell.

Ten minutes and five more rings later—and no sign of activity from within—Lawrence places a call to police dispatch to get someone out here to do a 'wellness check.' Legally, we can't break in... but the police can.

While we wait for them, we check with Betty's neighbors. One's not home, the other hasn't seen her in a while, and points out that her car—an old Impala—is still there. The cops arrive in about eight minutes. Between the buildup of mail, no response to knocking, the car sitting there, and Betty approaching seventy years old, they decide to make entry.

Officer Stark, a short guy with a bodybuilder physique, pulls a small wand-like device off his belt, which zaps the lock open in a flash of glowing yellow light. He pulls the door open and peers in. "Mrs. Reed? Ugh. What's that smell?"

Lawrence and I exchange 'aww damn' looks.

"Nasty is what it is," says Officer Fuentes, following him in. She gags within seconds. "Doesn't smell like a body."

I head in after the cops, Lawrence behind me.

The smell is sadly familiar.

"We're too late," I say.

Both cops look at me.

"That smell... same thing in the air at two past fires."

We find what's left of Betty Reed scattered around the toilet of the upstairs bathroom. Both lower legs remain fairly intact from mid-shin down, still in pink slippers. Her arms are nearly whole, one on either side of the bowl, but everything else has reduced to a dense black ashy sludge that stinks just like the other two victims—a mixture of spoiled milk, corpse, char, and that earthy mushroom aroma.

"Little too much jalapeño?" asks Fuentes.

"Takes a bit more than jalapeño to get this hot," I say. "Maybe that reaper pepper."

"Bed's been slept in." Officer Stark grimaces at the scene in the bathroom. "Probably woke up in the middle of the night."

Lawrence studies the swath of black stretching up the wall behind the toilet to the ceiling. Though, it's less a char mark and more a stain from greasy smoke, like someone sprayed tar on the wall. "Same thing as the last two."

"I'm going to skip the psychic stuff here unless you really want me to look. Pretty sure I don't want to watch this one." I look at the cops. "You guys have any problem if I hunt around downstairs for where she got the produce from?"

"Produce?" asks Stark.

I explain my theory that some magically-tainted vegetables are responsible for at least three deaths.

Stark emits a subdued chuckle. "Maybe my kid's got a point about not eating his broccoli."

"That shit'll kill ya," says Fuentes.

"So you guys have any problem with me looking around?" I ask.

"Umm. Probably not too big an issue." Fuentes waves me to follow her.

We head downstairs. I first check the kitchen and fridge, but strike out. Mrs. Reed's purse is on a small table next to a rune oven. Some people keep receipts, so I gently rummage it. Fuentes walks up beside me.

"Just looking for receipts."

"You really penised the chief's car?"

I laugh. "Yep. Though that was Brooklyn 1.0. I'm slightly more mature now with slightly better self-control. Now, I'd use stick-on cling film dicks. No destruction of property there and still funny."

"Nice." Fuentes edges over and peers into the sink. "Hey, check this."

The purse has enough tissues to handle an influenza outbreak in a small Central American country, but no receipts. I abandon it and head over to the sink. Black scorch marks and a few tiny bits of charcoal litter the bottom.

"That's weird," I say.

"Is that your professional arson investigator's opinion?"

I shrug. "I'm just a firefighter… Lawrence is the arson guy. But, I'm psychic, so I help out with the bizarre ones."

"No kidding…" She chuckles. "If you're psychic, how come you got arrested so much as a kid?"

"Ugh. If I had a dollar for every time I hear that now. Not that kind of psychic. I read stuff out of objects. No future-seeing for this girl." No, I'm not going to tell her I can peek into minds and sorta compel people to do stuff. Some things I just don't tell the cops, even if I *am* trying to be a good girl. And it is kind of annoying how all the cops just know me. Then again, there aren't a whole lot of female firefighters around here.

"Oh, that's cool. My sister's into that Ouija board stuff."

Officer Fuentes rattles on about her sister for the next forty five minutes or so while I roam around the house looking for any sign of where Mrs. Reed got those veggies. I even call Emerson and ask him to check her credit card purchases for anything that looks like it could've been food. By the time I'm off the phone with him, the cops have a forensics crew in here as a matter of procedure.

Lawrence collects me soon after and brings me outside. "Not much more we can do here. The police are taking over this scene for the moment. Even with what you've so far discovered, I'm stuck calling this one an accident. One more stop if you're up for it."

"Sure, why not?"

We head back to his truck. Within seconds of me getting in, I receive a text from Tracy asking if I can take Ash tonight. I send back a ‹Sure, but still at work. Check w Nat and lmk. If she can't, I'll ask Mom. Will pick her up from Nat when I'm off work.›

She replies with ‹K.›

Lawrence drives to Marvine Street, where Mr. and Mrs. Perez

lived, only two houses away. "Here. Found out from the police that Mrs. Perez and the woman who lives here were fairly close. No relation, but they supposedly spent a lot of time together."

"Okay."

We approach another row house. This time, Lawrence hits the bell.

A woman answers, late twenties or early thirties, still wearing a nice grey skirt suit and makeup like she hasn't been home from a cushy office job for much more than a few minutes yet. "Can I help you?"

I catch a whiff of smoke in the air.

"Mrs. Machado?" Lawrence takes a moment to introduce us. "We're investigating what happened with your friend, Ana Perez."

"Oh, poor Ana." The woman looks down. "They said she died in a fire, but the house doesn't look like anything happened. It's so strange. And please, call me Rosa."

"Speaking of fire," I say, "did something burn in your house recently?"

The sorrow flees from her expression, replaced with annoyance. "Oh, my son set off a firecracker in the trashcan. I can't believe what got into him."

Lawrence blinks. "A firecracker in the trash? Boys do have a fondness for things that explode, but that's a rather odd place to set one off."

"Who knows what made him do it?" Rosa grumbles. "He probably lit it right before I caught him with it and tossed it in there to hide it. Went off right next to me!"

"Did the trash catch fire?" I ask.

"A little. I put it out." She looks up at us. "Maybe you two could talk some sense into him, scare him into never doing anything like this again. He isn't listening to me, so hearing it from the fire department might be different. Come in, please." She scurries inside calling out for Daniel.

"Might as well. An excuse to look around." Without waiting for Lawrence's reaction, I follow and bee-line for the kitchen.

The smell of burn is stronger the deeper into the house I go, mixing with a tomato-soupy fragrance that's making me hungry as hell. A molten wreck of a formerly-white plastic trashcan stands at the end of the kitchen counter. The bottom's swollen out, split into strands like molten cheese. Ashy water's all over the floor at the base, and the mop that Rosa had likely been using to clean it up when we rang the doorbell is in the sink.

"That doesn't look like a firecracker." Lawrence peers into the can. "More like someone dropped a wad of burning rags into the garbage."

"Could it have been a sparkler or something that burns slow?"

He shrugs. "Possible. Too far burned to tell. But it wasn't an m80 type thing. That would've blasted the can apart into sharp fragments."

Rosa returns with a skinny boy of about ten, though his rounded face and large eyes make him look younger. If I only saw a portrait, I'd guess him to be closer to seven. He trudges in, staring at the floor like he's being led to his execution. The boy's a little too tall for me to squat down to eye level with—I'd be looking up at him if I did that, so I don't. I do, however, try to sound comforting.

"Hey, Daniel. Can you tell me what happened here?"

He looks up, makes eye contact, and starts crying. "I don't know. The garbage just exploded. I swear I didn't have any fireworks. Mama doesn't believe me, but I didn't do it."

There's no guilt as far as I can pick up off his surface thoughts... he's mostly hurt that his mother doesn't believe him. I lean on his brain, peering in as deep as I can. He's picturing himself sitting at the kitchen table doing homework when the trashcan spontaneously ignited. It freaked him out.

"Tell the firefighters what you did," says Rosa.

I hold up a hand. "I'm actually inclined to believe your son here."

"What?" Rosa blinks at me.

The boy's face lights up with hope. "I don't know what happened. The trash just caught fire."

"I'm mildly psychic. Your son really doesn't know what happened to the trash. He's not radiating any guilt at all."

Rosa's anger fades. "It really isn't like him to lie... I thought he was afraid of getting in trouble."

"What was in the trash before it went up?" I ask.

"Umm. Not much. I just filled the previous bag and took it out while cooking. A couple of paper towels, pasta box, and some vegetable scraps."

"Vegetable scraps." Lawrence raises both eyebrows at me.

"Mostly potato skins and carrot shavings." Rosa gestures at a pot on the stove. "I'm making soup."

I approach the pot and lift the lid, sniffing at a lovely vegetable soup heavy on the tomato. "This smells amazing."

"Thank you," says Rosa with a hint of confusion.

A floating hunk of potato gives me a weird tingle in the brain when I look at it. Oh, that's got magical energy in it. These people can't eat this. Unconcerned with being sanitary, I reach two fingers into the boiling soup and pluck out that potato nugget.

Rosa gasps. "Umm…"

"Whoa," mutters Daniel. "Careful, you'll burn yourself."

"This is giving off an odd energy."

Rosa just stares at me.

I hurl the potato hunk at the floor. It explodes on contact, creating a volleyball-sized sphere of flames.

"Holy crap!" yells Daniel, before darting behind his mother.

"Going out on a limb here, but"—I pluck and toss another bit of potato, which also explodes—"as good as this smells, you probably shouldn't eat it."

"But…" Rosa looks at Lawrence.

He shakes his head. "If you eat that soup, you're most likely going to die in your sleep from a slow internal burn."

She shivers. "Like Ana…"

"On second thought…" Lawrence walks over and turns the stove off. "I think we should take the soup for evidence. It exceeds safety levels for spiciness."

"Oh my." Rosa stares at the small round dark spot where the potato chunks blew up. She pales, nearly reaching my shade of white.

"Do you remember where you got these vegetables from?" I ask.

"Yes. Dierdorff's," says Rosa. "I always get my vegetables from there if I can. It's a family farmer's market just outside Doylestown. They don't use any chemicals."

"Heck of a ride for veggies." Lawrence puts the lid back on the pot.

"I swear by them." Rosa folds her arms, shaking her head. "I've never had vegetables explode before. Do you think the farm is doing it on purpose? They're always talking about how they don't use chemicals. I thought it was safe."

I pick up the pot. "It's too early to tell, but we'll go ask them."

# 15

## ATTACK OF THE KILLER POTATOES

After a brief stop at Lawrence's office to drop the deadly soup at the lab, we head up to Doylestown. I'm going way past my shift, but this literally is a case of life and death. On the ride up, I call Natalie to follow up on the Ashley situation.

Of course, the kid's thrilled to hang out at the enchanter shop, especially early enough that she can go swimming in Natalie's pool. Maybe that kid does need some psychological help. Who wants to swim in October?

I explain the situation with the exploding vegetables to Natalie. "So, do you have any idea why cutting, cooking, or chewing them isn't causing pyrotechnics, but they're sometimes igniting on their own and blowing up in response to sharp impact?"

"You're asking magic to obey the laws of logical reasoning." Natalie laughs. "Oh, sorry. I shouldn't laugh if people are dying. Umm. Well, from what you've said it sounds like—"

"Fix her rune oven before it kills us all!" shouts Ashley in the background.

That gets me giggling.

"Hah. Okay. So, yeah... based on what you said, I think cutting the veggies open is probably starting some kind of timer that causes combustion based on the amount of vegetable matter involved. Like those potato peels went off pretty quick in the trashcan. Chewing... I dunno. My best guess is not enough shock. And who knows what effect stomach acid had on it."

I roll my head around to stretch my neck. Too much time in cars today. "Does something like this sound deliberate?"

"Might be, but there's so many variables that could go wrong here it can't be targeted at specific people. You're probably looking for the mage equivalent of someone who tampers with crap in a store trying to hurt random people. Or maybe it's an unintended side effect of growth potions or pesticide magic. That farm claiming not to use chemicals doesn't mean they're not trying to do the same thing magically."

"That's a thought. Thanks. Tell Ash I... might be home in about two hours."

"Oh, she should be asleep by then."

I sigh. Damn. I was kinda looking forward to hanging with the kid. After everything going on, I need a shot of childishness. "Sorry. Can't exactly walk away from this investigation. People are at risk."

"Oh, it's cool. She understands. Already had a talk with her about it."

"Nice. Okay. Gotta go. Thanks, Nat."

"No problem."

Lawrence looks over at me. "What's the good word from the magic expert?"

"If someone's doing this on purpose, they're throwing crap out there trying to hit random victims. Or, it's an accident with whatever enchanted substances Dierdorff's farm is using on their crops so they can technically say they don't use chemicals."

"Think we should have a state trooper meet us out there?"

"Nah. Not just yet. This could be an accident. If the dude is dirty, I'm pretty sure I can handle a farmer."

"Heh." Lawrence shifts his weight. "You'll understand if I hang back a little. I just got out of the hospital."

"That's fine. In fact, please do." I pat him on the shoulder. "I don't want you to be hurt again."

"Works for me." He emits a wheezy chuckle. "I don't want to be hurt again. The food at the hospital ain't the best."

We pull into a dirt parking lot past a large wooden sign bearing the words 'Dierdorff's Farm.' A wide one-story building abuts the parking area, half of it consisting only of a roof over a concrete slab full of tables. They probably hold produce when the place is open, but at nearly 8 p.m., they're barren.

A vast swath of farmland stretches off behind the place, reminding me a bit of where I grew up. Not used to seeing so much open space since moving to Philly. Several tractors and some other farm equipment I have no idea what to call sit in a row off to the right. The machinery doesn't look new, but it's far from run-down.

I hop out of the SUV and approach the left half of the building that's an enclosed store, peering in the glass door at a dark room full of shelves. A shadow moves in the back end of the room, so I decide to knock.

A thick-bodied guy with a fat brown mustache emerges from a hallway. He can't be too much older than thirty and appears simultaneously muscular and paunchy. Wouldn't call the guy fat, but he's not hurting for food.

"Hey." I wave. "Got a minute?"

The man sets a crate down and walks over. "Sorry, we're closed. Doors lock at six."

I pat at my belt in search of a badge I'm not wearing, then reach out to my left, grab Lawrence's ID hung around his neck, and hold it up. "We're not here to shop. Can we ask you a few questions?"

"You don't look like cops."

I smile. "That's because we're not. We're with the fire department."

"Oh." He undoes the lock and steps outside. "What's the Philly FD want with me?"

"I can't answer that without knowing who I'm speaking with." Lawrence smiles and offers a hand. "Lawrence Ellis, Philadelphia FD Arson Unit."

"Henry Dierdorff. No fancy title." He smiles and shakes hands.

"This your father's place?" I ask.

"Was. He's retired. I'm the owner now." Henry hooks his thumbs in his pockets, giving off simultaneous pride and exhaustion.

"Do you use any magical substances on your farm? Growth enhancement, pest stuff? Anything like that?"

"Nah." He shakes his head. "We're strictly natural, the way produce was meant to be grown. No chemicals, no potions, no spells. About the only thing we do differently from centuries ago is usin' tractors and machinery instead of hand-picking everything."

He's not being deceptive or defensive, unless my ability to read a person's intent has decided to flake out. I shift my demeanor from investigator to concerned friend. "Henry, there have been some... strange incidents involving produce that came from this farm. I'm pretty sure you have nothing to do with it or even any awareness of the situation. Three people so far that we know about have died as a direct result of consuming tainted vegetables. One couple narrowly avoided death because their cat knocked a bowl of veggies off the counter—and they exploded."

"Exploded?" Henry stares at me in shock.

"Yes. When subjected to a sharp impact, the tainted vegetables detonate. An inch-long bit of potato made a fireball the size of my head."

"Damn..." He whistles, shaking his head. "Are you sure it came from here?"

"Reasonably. One person who had some of the tainted produce mentioned she bought it here, but I'd like to look around a bit if that's okay."

He nods, worry clear in his expression. "All right. What are you hoping to find?"

"Anything out of the ordinary. Glowing energy, used-up wands, something of that nature," says Lawrence.

"Or a psychic impression." I flash a cheesy smile. "That's why I think you're as much a victim in this situation as the people who smoldered away to ashes in their sleep. I can tell you have nothing to do with this."

"Shit. Okay. C'mon in." Dierdorff relaxes visibly and leads us into the shop.

I go straight to the stacks of produce piled against the wall, the same boxes that probably sat out on the tables all day for sale. The oddity I felt off the soup is ten times stronger here. I pick up a spud and my entire hand prickles with energy.

Eyes closed, I try to 'read' it. A needling sense of something lurks slightly out of my reach. That tells me whoever is responsible for tainting the vegetables had little emotional involvement in the act. Or maybe it's not the work of a person as much as a magical creature.

"This whole box of potatoes is dangerous." I hand the one I'm holding to Lawrence. "Does that feel strange to you at all? Tingles or anything?"

He looks it over, shrugs, shakes his head, and hands it to Dierdorff.

"Feels fine." Henry offers it back to me.

Based on what a small piece did, I'm not going to 'impact test' this spud inside. "I should go outside for this."

"For what?" asks Henry.

"Proof." I walk out to a good twenty yards from the building in the middle of the dirt parking lot.

Henry and Lawrence follow.

I throw the potato at the ground aiming for a spot about ten feet away. It blows up with enough of a concussion wave to throw me on my back and leave me staring at a few new stars that aren't part of the sky. Though it feels like an instant before Lawrence and Henry are standing over me, I have a feeling I lost some time.

"Ouch," I mutter. "Wasn't expecting it to be *that* big."

"That potato just exploded," says Henry in a somewhat robotic tone.

"Yep."

Lawrence helps me up. "How many are affected?"

"That entire box felt tainted. If something hits it hard enough, the whole building is going to be toothpicks."

"Shit." Henry spits off to the side. "What the hell did this?"

"That's what I'm trying to figure out. Need to look around a bit more. Got a weak hit off that tater, but couldn't see anything."

"Okay." Henry points at a small green pickup with a row of spotlights on the roof. "We can check the fields."

"Sounds like a decent idea. Where are the potatoes?"

Henry drives us out about a third of a mile into the field and pulls over by rows of squat, green leafy plants. I head off into the patch, trying to keep my supernatural feelers open for anything like what I felt from the potato that knocked me on my ass. Lawrence and Henry follow, both with flashlights—which is awesome because it's damn dark out here.

Once we near the middle of the area, a trace of energy in the air leads me to a swath of plants that all give off weird vibes. I crouch and gently grasp some leaves, again attempting to pull a vision out of them.

A few minutes of high concentration gets me nowhere but eager to go home. Yeah, I never did deal with frustration well. It's one of the big reasons I ignored competitive sports in school. It's a good thing that my job saving the world requires me to do nothing at all. To prevent total destruction, I merely plant my ass on my couch. That's right up my alley. If I had to chase down some revved up Elestari and out-über them, the world would be in deep shit.

I stand, grumbling. "Nah. Nothing. Whatever happened here didn't leave a strong enough imprint. No emotional investment in doing this."

"Hey, Amari?" asks Lawrence. "Have a look at this."

The urge to stop wasting time and go home is strong, but I bite it back. People have died. People will continue to die. And this bothers me why? Okay, they're not *bad* people. And Ashley would probably not like it if I let random humans keep dying. Or, I dunno. The kid's got a little bit of a dark streak. I mean, on some level, she does believe she summoned me—a demon—to kill her mother's ex-boyfriend. It's doubtful she suspected his true intention toward her. More likely, she wanted the asshole to stop beating the shit out of her mother.

Natalie, however, would pout at me for letting harmless old people burn in their sleep. And okay, that Daniel kid came within inches of the same fate. This random potato bomb bullshit could affect kids.

Oh, okay fine. I walk over to Lawrence. "What'cha got?"

"Glass bottle. Caught a glint off the flashlight." He points.

I crouch and peer at an unlabeled beer bottle. "Looks like someone was drinking out here."

"Don't usually have people hanging out in my fields," says Henry. "Most of my workers are family. The handful of employees who aren't related ain't old enough to drink yet. Mostly part timers in school."

"Suppose I can try..." I stick a finger in the opening at the top, figuring it the least likely place for any fingerprints to exist should this be important, then try to reach out with my psychic feeler.

Something lurks in the bottle, stronger than the nuclear potato. Trying to read it feels like I'm walking into a standing wall of plastic wrap and bouncing off. The imprint is nowhere near as strong as the psychic residue I found in the ashes, but then again, emotions don't get much more powerful than at the moment a person dies—or when they're stuck behind some moron driving thirty-five less than the speed limit.

Speaking of emotion, I tap into frustration for a little boost... and pierce the shrink wrap.

The vision I pop into appears to be the same field at night. While I can't tell exactly how far back in the past this is, the potato plants don't look too much smaller than they are now. A shadowy figure walks closer to where I'm 'floating.' A shift in the clouds lets the moonlight briefly reveal the lines of a nice business suit and a dark ball cap. I guess he figured if he's going to sneak somewhere at night, he might as well commit a fashion crime. The guy's on the larger end of average in size, but there isn't enough light for me to make out much about what he looks like other than probably being a white dude.

He reaches into his suit coat and pulls the bottle out, full of glowing sky-blue liquid. The light makes it pretty obvious he's got gloves on. So much for prints. Plant by plant, he dribbles the stuff into the soil, keeping low as if afraid someone in the distance might see the luminous bottle. The way he's creeping around is a pretty clear sign he's not the Miracle Gro fairy come to do random good deeds. He's definitely up to some shady shit. When he's maybe six feet away from me, he trips, hurling the bottle involuntarily on his way to French kiss the dirt. The last of the potion flies out of the bottle when it lands, seeping into the ground and going dark.

"Shit," rasps the man, scrambling back up into a crouch.

After a few seconds holding completely still, he seems to trust that no one heard him fall and starts searching around for the empty bottle. At a distant dog bark, the guy gives up and runs off into the next plot where he can hide in the taller plants.

I fade back to reality and lift the bottle up, impaled on the finger I stuck in the top. "Here's your problem."

"What did you see?" asks Mr. Dierdorff.

"Some dude was sneaking around here pouring some kind of glowing blue potion on the ground. I'm no mage, but I'm pretty sure it's the reason you're growing weapons-grade spuds."

Dierdorff clenches his hands in fists. "Browning. It had to be Browning… or someone working for him."

"Who is this 'Browning' person and what makes you suspect him?" Lawrence pulls out his notepad. "Have you had problems with him in the past?"

"Yeah, but nothing like this. Nothing so… illegal." He shakes his head, grumbling to himself. "Browning works for a corporate farm not too far from here, Hearthwood Gardens Farms."

"I've heard of them." Lawrence jots on his pad. "In the news a lot over that labor thing with the constructs."

"Right." Dierdorff nods. "They've been trying to buy up or shut down any other farms around here bigger than a back yard. Bring in their big name and their enchanted machines, get rid of paid employees. Of course, they assure me that I'll still have a place with their company… but I don't trust it as far as I can throw one of those walking monstrosities."

A long sigh leaks out of my throat. "I hate golems."

Dierdorff looks at me. "Does that psychic stuff work in court? Can you nail him for this?"

"Psychic testimony can be used for corroboration but doesn't often stand on its own." Lawrence taps the pen on the paper while thinking. "Unless we can get something like security camera footage of him trespassing or tampering with your crops, or maybe fingerprints on the bottle, we'll need more than Brooklyn's word."

"No prints. He had gloves."

"So... I'm still stuck?" Dierdorff looks about ready to explode himself.

Damn. Night's already shot to hell. Might as well make it a little longer. I point around with the bottle still hanging off my finger. "So, where is this guy? Maybe we can go talk to him."

"What are you hoping to do there?" asks Lawrence.

"Just confirm that he is or is not involved. I should be able to get a read on him. If he's got nothing to do with it, no sense wasting time investigating him." I smile at Dierdorff. "So, where is he?"

Dierdorff starts tromping off back toward his truck. "Come on. I'll drive you."

"Hold on a moment," calls Lawrence while jogging after him. "Better you stay here. If that man *is* involved, things will stay calmer if we appear neutral. Your being there will create the appearance of bias."

"All right. Fine." He stops and points. "Take a right out of the front lot, then the third left onto Sunflower Road. It's about five minutes down. Enormous place. Can't miss it."

"Okay. Thanks." I hand over the bottle. "The tampering with your crops is something the police will need to look into. They have psychics, too. Might need to show them this."

Dierdorff takes it and nods. "Be careful over there. Dangerous group."

"Mob?" I ask.

"Worse," says Dierdorff. "Corporation."

# 16

# HEARTHWOOD GARDENS

Lawrence hops in the department SUV and spends a moment staring out the windshield.

"You okay?" I ask.

A wistful smile spreads over his face. "Yeah, just savoring the last few minutes I have to enjoy the ability to walk and breathe on my own before winding up in the hospital again."

"We're only going to talk to this guy."

Lawrence teases his finger around the start button. "I recall a similar sentiment when we visited that house."

"We're not going through a portal this time." I grin. "But if you want to wait here, that's fine. I can hop over there myself."

He hits the button and drops the SUV into reverse. "I'm mostly teasing. Not like we're chasing after a mage."

"Normal people don't brew potions of exploding potato."

Lawrence gives me major side eye.

"Of course, he could've bought it from an alchemist. His *pouring* magic gunk on a farm plot doesn't prove he made it."

"Right... You're trying to take away my nice retirement." He chuckles, shaking his head. "If that guy *is* a mage, my ass is staying right here in the truck."

I nod. "Good."

"This really ought'a be something the cops do."

"You're right. I'm only trying to make sure we sic the cops on the right person. Dierdorff seems to have a grudge."

A fireball goes up into the air from behind the store as we pull off onto the road. Lawrence jams on the brakes with a startled yelp.

"What the hell was—"

*Boom. Boom. Boom.*

"Looks like he's disposing of the tainted produce. At least that's one problem out of the way, assuming he keeps checking things before people go foom in the night."

Lawrence takes a few breaths before continuing to drive. "There still could be tainted produce out there in smaller stores yet. Maybe even other farms involved if what that guy said is true."

"Could be. But we still don't know if Hearthwood is doing this. Honestly, it sounds a little out there. Why would a big corporate farm sabotage Dierdorff's? I mean, his operation is pretty damn big but it can't be that much of a threat. Some random guy doing random evil shit is more likely." I scowl at a sudden realization. "Hey, you remember that gas pipeline fire the other week?"

"Yeah. Damn what a mess. Amazing more people didn't get hurt."

"No kidding. I think it might've been deliberate sabotage. A chemical plant in Jersey had a suspicious lightning strike start a fire. And then some guys at a logging camp all died to lightning. Maybe there's some kind of, I dunno, eco-mage-terrorist running around?"

"Why would an eco-terrorist attack a farm that prides itself on being organic?" He sneaks a quick smile at me before making a left turn.

I let my head fall back against the seat. "Ugh. Right. And there's no lightning involved here."

Eco-terrorists. Right. I really don't need to be trying to come up with more work for myself. Not my problem if someone wants to blow up industry. Well, I suppose it *is* my problem if they start a fire within five miles of my station house, but... yeah. I'm not gonna make *more* extra work for myself.

A moment after that thought dances across my brain, a brilliant white glow rises up from the dark expanse of vegetation up ahead. Beneath a dark indigo sky, a dome of brilliant artificial light surrounds a massive farm complex. Dozens of hulking humanoid figures lumber around in the fields, entirely in silhouette except for bright green eye spots. All look about twelve feet tall, though they vary in bulk. Some skinny with long gangly arms, others thicker. The army of mindless workers moves in near synchronicity, as if one person had a remote control that operated them all at once.

"What in the name of..." Lawrence stares.

"Somehow I doubt I'm going to put one of those golems down with a single punch to the forehead," I mutter.

We keep driving. Heavy thuds shake the ground on both sides from unseen automatons working in total darkness. The intense light is concentrated on the main building at the center of the farm compound, a long single-story warehouse almost as big as a city block. Guess the enchanted workforce doesn't need light to see. When we reach the entrance to the parking lot, Lawrence stops only a few yards inside. Only one other car is here, a black Beemer sitting by a door on the largest building.

"It's gettin' on about nine-thirty," says Lawrence. "You think that guy's going to be here at this hour?"

"Probably not... unless he *is* running around at night with strange potions. The place is in operation though. Someone's gotta be here to manage, right?"

"In theory." Lawrence parks next to the Beemer. "I'll observe from here."

"Am I overstepping the boundaries of an arson investigation?"

"A little, but I'm curious to see where this goes. Even the cops hate dealing with the magic ones, so I'm sure they won't mind you doing their work for them... to a point."

I hop out. "Right. Don't do anything I can't talk my way out of going to jail for."

"Something like that." He winks.

Grinning, I head over to the warehouse door on the other side of the Beemer. It's got a buzzer, so I push it. A startled male shout comes from inside. Guess he's not used to having visitors at this hour.

My phone pings with a ‹Where are you?› from Natalie, followed by ‹U ok?›

I'm in the middle of sending ‹Yeah, still at work. Sorry.› when the door opens.

"Uhh, we're closed," says a man.

"Sec." I hit send, then look up.

A mid-forties dude with salt and pepper hair and a Hearthwood Gardens Farms green polo shirt leans out the half open door. He's tall and broad shouldered, but neither muscular nor bookish.

"Hey." I smile. "I'm Brooklyn Amari with the Philadelphia Fire Department. Sorry to bother you so late, but I'm investigating some unusual fires. Can I ask your name?"

"Ted Browning. I'm the general manager of this farm." The intent the guy's giving off shifts from 'go the hell away' to 'oh shit,' though his facial expression doesn't change.

Crap. Seriously? Dierdorff's *right?*

"What's that have to do with Hearthwood?" asks Browning.

"Oh, just standard procedure checking with farms in the area for tampering. Seems we've got a kook out there sneaking around at night and pouring some manner of potion into the ground that's turning potatoes into bombs. We've had three confirmed deaths so far."

Browning's eyebrows go up. "That's horrible. I haven't seen any intrusion alarms. We've got sensors all over the property and the tenders react to unauthorized persons in the field."

The read I'm getting off him now is part way between a strong urge to destroy/hide something and wanting to hurry me off the property. Yeah, he's throwing off guilt the way I did when I had a half pound of Khadafy weed in my purse and cop grabbed me at the mall for shoplifting. In hindsight, it had been really stupid to shoplift with that much pot. But that top was *so* cute. Anyway, I bet he's going to run straight to his stock of potions and dump them down the toilet before the cops arrive. Ooh. You know I bet that bag of weed is *still* in the ceiling in that store's 'loss protection' office. Love telekinesis. And no... I didn't lose money on it. You know how pissed off drug dealers get when their product floats out a window?

Actually, I'm not sure. He never saw me. But I bet he was pretty pissed.

"React? I'm guessing the 'tenders' are those giant robots?"

"They're not robots." He smiles. "They're constructs. All locally sourced enchanters. Hearthwood Gardens Farms does try to do right by the community. No Chinese-made golems here."

"Right... what exactly would they do if someone trespassed?"

Browning smiles. "Oh, they only make a lot of noise and light. They are non-violent."

"Mind if I ask why the general manager is here so late at night?"

He shrugs. "Big shipment coming together for tomorrow morning. I wanted to make sure nothing went wrong."

Okay, the guy is pretty slick. Without my mental abilities, I really can't say I'd have caught that as a lie. I stare into his eyes, concentrating on my desire to instill the concept of 'truth' into his mind.

"Do you know anything about the potions being poured on the Dierdorff farm?"

"The incendiary ones? No. I mean, they're expensive. Wait, how should I know? The potions are *probably* expensive. And they weren't supposed to kill anyone." He blinks at me. "Shit."

"So you *weren't* trying to kill people and set Dierdorff up for it?"

Browning looks me up and down. "You're not a cop."

"Nope. Firefighter."

He gives me a plastic smile and goes to slam the door in my face. I stall it an inch from closed with telekinesis. Browning struggles, pushing at the unmoving slab, but can't move it. He gives up and runs away.

I glance at Lawrence. "Okay, now would be a good time to call in the police. Be right back. He's going to destroy the evidence."

Browning disappears into a hallway on the other side of a modest reception area. I chase him past a couple conference rooms, around a corner, and into a huge open space filled with conveyor belts and flying boxes.

Enchanted, levitating blocks with arms glide back and forth carrying huge bins of produce. Enormous machines aglow with streamers of green, blue, and red light process various veggies. The very air *tastes* like magic in here. Browning's probably the only human in the entire place. He dashes past a hopper spitting tomatoes onto a belt heading for a shrink-wrap machine, grabs a pole to stop himself from falling over on a tight turn, and sprints into another corridor at the back end of the processing floor.

He skids to a stop at the end, keying in a code on a numeric pad. A heavy grey door beside it pops open with a magical chime two seconds before I can get to him. He ducks in and tries again to slam a door in my face, but in the heat of the moment, I boot it in.

Browning flies off his feet, landing on his back a short distance away in a room with three worktables and almost as much magical stuff as Natalie's place. Bottles, jars, weird loopy glass tubes full of bright purple liquid, and bowls of various powders and substances surround me. This looks like exactly the wrong place to have a fight— at least not without someone winding up polymorphed into a tie-dyed sheep.

"Somehow, I'm guessing 'please don't destroy the evidence' isn't going to work," I say.

With a groan, Browning throws himself over onto all fours, then rises onto his knees. He grabs the edge of a table for help standing, also grasping a mini-sledgehammer. The second he raises it to smash bottles, I telekinetically yank him toward me. He swings anyway, but the surprise of having nothing in the path of the hammer causes him to nearly flip himself over onto his back with the force he put behind the effort.

"Really, don't destroy this shit. The cops need to see it."

He points the hammer at me. "That's assault."

"What?" I shrug, flashing a go-screw-yourself smile. "I didn't lay a hand on you."

Growling, he starts for the table of glassware... and again, I drag him back with telekinesis. This time, I sidestep so I can fling him out into the hall. He flails his arms for balance, managing not to fall on his ass before his back hits the wall. With him out of the room, I stand in the doorway, blocking him.

"You spent many hours on timeout as a kid, didn't you? Not too good with listening."

A sudden, manic look flashes in his eyes. Oops. Looks like he's decided to try out that hammer on bone instead of glass. He raises the weapon, but I dash in at him before he can charge, grabbing his neck with my right hand and catching his elbow in my left, stalling his arm so he can't swing at me.

He stops struggling when I lift him off his feet by his throat, pressing him into the wall, his eyes nearly bulging out of their sockets.

"You're mixing potions, Ted. Not like you're clueless about magic. Don't be so surprised I'm stronger than I look."

Browning gurgles.

"Now, before this gets unpleasant, why don't we go outside and wait for the police?"

A shift in the ambient energy makes the hair on the back of my neck stand up. Great... what now?

Four tall, vertical clouds of dark red light appear, two on either side of us, slightly pointy at the top and bottom, and lighter in the middle. Browning's next gurgle has a hint of surprise to its tone. Okay, guess he's not doing this. I relax the pressure on his throat.

He wheezes. "What the fuck?"

"Was that directed at me or at whatever those clouds are?"

Before he can answer, a Shaar'Nath steps out of each vaporous mass, the shortest of the four about seven feet tall. Two have jet-black armor, one white like me, one crimson. All dudes this time. I can't help myself and burst into laughter.

The Shaar'Nath hesitate, the aggression in their eyes notching back to confusion at my wholly inappropriate reaction to their menacing glowers.

"What?" asks the biggest one, Mr. Crimson, who's nearly ten feet tall.

"You guys really oughta work on your entrance. Those energy clouds looked like giant vaginas."

Both black-armored ones grumble.

"Look, do we really have to do this?" I ask. "I'm kind of in the middle of something at the moment. Can we reschedule this for maybe an hour from now?"

All four of them extend their claws.

"Guess not."

Browning screams, wets himself, and faints.

Cool. I drop him. Don't have to worry about him breaking shit while I'm having my ass kicked.

# 17

## AN ILL-CONCEIVED PLAN

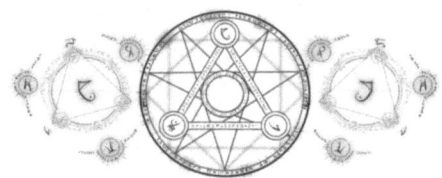

Four Shaar'Nath step closer to me, limiting my potential escape to the room full of potion supplies or trying to smash through a concrete wall.

I sigh, and shift myself all the way... once again grateful Natalie's amulet spares my uniform. Though I gain two feet of height, I'm still only even with the smallest of them.

Mr. Crimson points at Browning while eyeing Mr. White. "Kill that one, and shred this whole place."

The white one steps in to grab Browning while Big Red reaches for me. I let out a war cry, and kick a field goal into Mr. White's face as he bends down to grab the unconscious human. My foot launches him into the ceiling, but costs me avoiding Mr. Crimson's grab. He clamps his enormous hands around my arms at the elbow, pinning them to my sides like he's containing a ten-year-old who tried to pick a fight with a grown man.

Distracting him with seemingly aimless kicking and screaming, I swing my tail up and slice the onyx blade at the end into his groin. He lets out a deep, resonant bellow, loses his grip on me, and collapses into a flying ostrich pose, holding himself. The two black-armored Shaar'Nath rush at me simultaneously, but I take the opening in front of me and run—while telekinetically dragging Browning into my arms.

Carrying him like a giant football, I haul ass down the corridor, trying to remember which way to go. Not that I expect these guys will disappear the instant I'm outside, but maybe they'll hesitate at risking someone seeing them. Mostly, I want to get into view of the dash camera in Lawrence's truck so I'm clearly outside if/when this place is torn to shreds. Seems like they're looking to set me up for killing this dude. Great. With my juvenile record, it really wouldn't look good for me.

At a grunt of exertion close behind, I duck, covering Browning with my wings.

One of the black Shaar'Nath sails over me and plows face-first into the wall, crushing cinder blocks. Mr. White grabs my wing as I stand up, trying to pull me aside to get at the human. I spin toward him, taking a stabbing tail to my side so it doesn't hit Browning. The blade only goes in an inch or two, but it stings like a forty-pound wasp. Ouch, shit that hurts. No wonder Mr. Crimson is still cradling his non-balls.

I hammer my fist into Mr. White's jaw, sending him staggering at the wall, then yank the sixteen-inch blade from my armor plate. Out of spite, I hammer it into the floor as deep as I can. The two black-armored guys dive at me. One, nearly flying, wraps his arms around my upper body while Mr. White obligingly staggers into the path of the second, causing a painfully loud collision. The one who hit me knocks me flat to the ground and sliding under his much greater weight. Browning's somewhere between us doing a performance art piece entitled *The Human Pancake.*

I didn't hear any bones crack, so he's probably okay.

We hit the wall, denting another hole in the cinderblocks. Tall Black picks me up like a rag doll, Browning rolling limp to the side. The dude's eyes, glowing pools of green energy, lock with mine for two seconds before I kick him as hard as I can in the groin.

He bounces a little, but otherwise doesn't react. I hang in his grip flashing a cheesy grin. Somewhere in the back of my mind, I remember Dad saying I'm more powerful than them here in the Armistice, but with such a size disparity between us, I can't help but feel at a disadvantage.

I kick him again, and he gives me an unimpressed smirk.

"Really?" He tilts his head.

Okay, I know my nether bits disappear when I armor up—at least it kinda feels like I'm wearing Kevlar pants over them. The guys have the same featureless-flat crotch as me, not even a bulge. Wonder if they do like a cat thing and it can retract? If not, no wonder they're so violent... talk about 'too tight.'

"Hey... does your junk like disappear into a pocket dimension when you shift up, or is it all squished in there under the plate? I mean, it's probably not *that* small... shouldn't there be a bulge at least?"

He looks down at himself... giving me the perfect opportunity to ram my knee up into his forehead. Tall Black falls away from me and I drop back to my feet—right as Mr. White and Short Black jump over him. Damn. Guess the tail-in-the-floor thing didn't hold him long.

I play goalie as best I can, trying to keep them away from Browning, who's *still* unconscious behind me. While I've never had any formal instruction for hand to hand combat, I've been in plenty of scraps. Amid a blur of claws, fangs, and gleaming onyx tail blades, I'm sure this looks more like a high school grudge brawl than anything else—only with less hair pulling and ripped clothes.

Kinda hard to rip clothes when everyone's naked.

Well, technicalities. Change that to 'kinda hard to rip clothes when everyone's in Kevlar bodysuits.'

Mr. White shreds a bit of my wing membrane—and that hurts so fucking much I scream my throat raw. Of course, being the sweet innocent girl I am, I pay him back by going all bad kitty on his wing, biting and tearing a three-foot strip of leathery black skin away.

I swear the man shrieks like a baby. He collapses, cradling the wing and... wow is he crying? Good, fucker. That's what you get.

Mr. Crimson *finally* gets to his feet and tromps up behind the brawl, limping. Black blood coats the inside of both his thighs, still pouring out the slice in his armor.

Short Black goes to punch me in the face, but I duck and ram an elbow into his gut. He doubles over, falling on top of me. A black tail tries to spear me in the chest, but I roll up on my side. The blade misses me by an inch and spears the floor behind me. I grab the tail, twist, and kick Tall Black in the side of the head. He flies from the force of impact until jerking to a stop by his stuck tail, then careening over for a face-first meeting with the floor, cracking the concrete.

Fortunately... or maybe unfortunately, I don't think Shaar'Nath can be knocked unconscious by a severe blow to the head. He lays there moaning. Mr. Crimson grabs Mr. White and peels him aside before seizing me with both hands around my throat. His desire for eye for an eye—or groin for a groin—is quite clear in his expression. I focus my telekinetic hold on the tail going for my crotch. The edge stops millimeters from my armor. He swings me to the side and bashes me into the wall, holding me there with his left arm while grabbing his tail in his other hand like a small sword.

Our slender tails don't have all that much strength—at least not compared to our arms. I'm not sure I can hold off his full strength with telekinesis alone... and it sure looks like he's intending to blur the line between a twenty-inch sword and a sex toy. Wow, Shaar'Nath really do have some dark kinks.

"Hey," I gurgle. "That box isn't for sharp object storage."

He growls.

Okay, maybe I started that particular grudge match. I mean, his crotch plate is still cut open and leaking blood, but hey... I slashed, not stabbed. The look in his glowing yellow eye pools tells me he's not going to stop with one thrust.

Shit.

I stare at the blade, waiting for the instant he jabs it at my groin. The second he strikes, I swing my hips to my right, kicking my left leg out and up over his shoulder as he drives his tail into the wall. After wrapping myself around the arm holding me, I swing my tail up, grab it like a knife, and slice the thumb off the hand at my throat.

Black blood sprays all over my face. He roars in a mixture of anger and pain, reaching at me with his intact hand. I kick out again for leverage and swing myself over from koala-hugging his arm to sitting on his shoulders with his face in my crotch. He doesn't take the time to enjoy it though... Mr. Crimson staggers to the side, raking at my lower back with his claws.

I grab his horns, shout, "Make a wish!" and yank.

The one in my right hand breaks off, giving me a ten-inch dagger that I promptly ram into the top of his head.

"Oops. Broke your horn. There. I put it back for you."

Mr. Crimson's body disintegrates into a cloud of fog. I flare my wings a little involuntarily as I drop back to my feet. Mr. White is inches from ripping Browning's throat out.

I launch myself into a flying tackle, dragging all three remaining Shaar'Nath to the ground. After a brief period of wild clawing at each other, we all seem to get tired of lying on the floor at the same time and stop fighting long enough to scramble upright.

"Hang on!" I shout.

The remaining three pause, evidently *just* noticing Mr. Crimson is gone. Hey, I did him a favor. Sure, it'll be awhile before he can go into the Armistice again, but at least he reintegrated in Imbreleth without a groin wound.

They stare at me.

"Okay... wait just a second." I raise my hands and take a step back, keeping myself between them and Browning. "Which side are you guys on: destroy the world or destroy me to protect the world?"

"What?" asks Short Black.

"Well... if you *want* me to destroy the world, exactly what purpose does trying to ruin my life serve?"

"Ruin your life?" asks Tall Black. "No, we're trying to stop you from destroying the Armistice."

Mr. White scratches his head.

"Wow, you guys are pretty dim... Okay, look. Big Red wanted you to kill that human behind me then rip up this whole place, right?"

All three of them nod.

"Framing me for murder, taking away my job and the life I have now is the exact *last* thing you should want to do. This is my home. If I have nothing left to lose and get seriously depressed…"

"Oh," says Mr. White. "Umm…"

I fold my arms. "And hey. Didn't my dad, I mean Baal'nethiel, tell you guys to leave me the hell alone? I hate being *that* girl, but if my dad finds out what you did, you're going to be in deep shit."

"Baal'nethiel said not to harm you." Tall Black shrugs. "Xirazh figured if you were in jail, you couldn't be manipulated."

"Not to harm me…" I glance at the bleeding stab wound in my side.

"You jumped in front of that." Short Black points at me.

"I didn't want you to kill that human."

They exchange glances.

"So you're a human lover now?" asks Mr. White.

"She's sleeping with one," whispers Short Black in a tone like he's telling them I do unseemly things to farm animals.

Tall Black gasps.

Mr. White glances at them. "What's wrong with that? I've had a few human women."

I sigh. "Not that I particularly like this guy, but I don't feel like being set up for murder. And do you *really* think that jail would slow me down?" I punch a hole in the cinder blocks with a halfhearted jab. "Seriously?"

Again they look at each other.

Mr. White fidgets, says, "Umm," then shrugs before disappearing in a cloud of crimson-black fog.

"Heh." Short Black laughs. "You're right. Those gates do kinda look like vaginas."

The two black-armored ones disappear amid noticeably rounder billows of energy.

"Ugh." I bow my head, face-palming. "The forces of evil are idiots. Wait. No, those guys are pro-Armistice. Guess they're more the 'forces of stupid.'"

Browning moans. I turn to look at him, cradling the stab wound in my lower left side. That's going to hurt for a couple days... Rapid footsteps echo from a corner a short distance away. Typical cops, always showing up just a little too late.

I shift back to normal, my armor, wings, tail, and horns disintegrating into whorls of black smoke that my body absorbs. Natalie's amulet puts my fire department uniform back on me, intact and un-smudged. My side still hurts, but doesn't appear to be actively bleeding. That would be rather obvious under a white polo shirt.

Six cops round the corner within seconds of my shapeshift finishing. They stop short, two nearly pulling their weapons as a reflex before they mentally process my uniform. Lawrence brings up the rear, looking around at the damaged walls

"What happened here?" asks the nearest cop.

I point at Browning, who still hasn't tried to sit up, then at the mini-sledge some thirty feet away down the hall. "He tried to destroy evidence. When I asked him not to, he attempted to take my head off."

The cops look around at the ripped up hallway. One whistles. All six give me incredulous looks.

"Oh, he didn't do that. Magic went haywire and like summoned some stuff. Browning fainted."

They look at me. Lawrence purses his lips and turns away so none of the cops can see his face. Two officers head over to check on Browning.

"Summoned something?" asks a blond guy, Officer Thompson.

"Not sure what they were. Claws, big... I grabbed Browning and ran like hell. We got lucky. The things seemed to really hate the walls more than us."

"Right..." Thompson looks me up and down. My immaculate uniform either confuses him or convinces him I didn't have anything to do with the destruction. "So, how'd you wind up in here?"

I sigh. "Short answer: Browning was tampering with the crops at a rival farm using potions that resulted in three deaths. The evidence is down there in that room. Might want to call in an arcane detective."

Browning lurches up to a sitting position and babbles incoherently. Seems like he blanked out the memory of seeing the four geniuses. Or maybe one of them gave him a brain whammy. A cop by the door to the potion lab lets out an impressed whistle.

"What about the long answer?" asks Thompson.

Damn. At this rate, I'm not even going to be able to go home tonight before I have to be at the station again.

# 18

## MORE ANGEL-DEMON STUFF

The next day sucked.

Three hours of sleep is shitty even for a half-demon.

In fact, the rest of the week is fairly high on the shit-o-meter. Not that anything new happened, but between sleep deprivation and worrying about Mom, I've been a mess. I did try and make it up to Ashley for disappearing on her by taking her to a science museum. For an eight-year-old, she's surprisingly understanding about my job pulling me away. A firefighter's a lot more life-and-death than an office drone. Then again, spending the day at Natalie's shop thrilled her so she didn't really mind.

Saturday finally arrives and I have super important plans for the entire weekend: I'm going to lounge around the apartment doing nothing. Time for a *me* day. This weekend, I will get my lazy on. Somewhere, I read that vegging out is good for the mind, so... yeah.

It's been awhile since I marathonned *Dead Like Me*, so... season one episode one, here we come. Still naked and damp from the shower, I flop on the couch to watch TV, idly brushing my fingers at where the tail got me. The bruise is almost gone, and it's only a little sore. My mood must be in the shitter since I'm not even interested in being around Jason. Nothing against him, just feeling the need to be alone for at least a day.

Just me and Ellen Muth.

Our 'friendship' could be even more intense if I got a Cinema Orb, but... bleh. I'm not dropping a few grand on a magical television, even if it is fully three-dimensional. And the media crystals are like $300 per movie. Bit pricey when the only advantage is having life-sized characters and scenes appearing in my living room. Okay, smelling stuff in movies is cool, but not $300 cool.

I let my tail out for no reason other than to swish it back and forth. After realizing I *have* one, I totally get why cats do that swishing thing when they want to be left alone. Granted, most cats couldn't cut a steel beam in half with their tail, but still. My onyx blade makes for good—intimidating—swishage.

By episode four, a twinge of hunger teases at my gut. In celebration of my lazy day, I order pizza. Even the effort of moving something from the freezer to the rune oven exceeds my tolerance for activity.

The doorbell rings about half an hour later. I pause the DVD and head to the door. I'm halfway across the room before I remember I'm naked, but lack the energy to care. Call the free show part of the driver's tip... assuming it's a guy.

I open the door—and then realize my tail's still showing. Fortunately, the guy, who can't be much older than twenty, is too mesmerized by the full-frontal to notice the wisp of shadow behind me as I put the death noodle away. He keeps staring as he hands me the receipt. I sign for the credit card purchase, give it back to him, and take the box from his hands like I'm sliding it out of a mannequin's grip.

"Thanks," I say.

The guy blinks, then grins. "Thanks! Have a great weekend."

I close the door, much to his disappointment, and head back to the sofa with my lunch-dinner. Once again, I flop on the sofa, my feet up on the coffee table in such an extreme slouch I'm basically lying flat.

Yeah, this is the life.

Of course, I'm enjoying the utter lack of doing anything—and this pizza—far too much, so it doesn't surprise me when Laniah appears in a cloud of silvery-white fog. She's wrapped in this airy white thing that makes her look more like a tree a bunch of kids TP'd for mischief night than a woman in a dress. Seriously, it's just a strip of fabric wrapped around her like a ribbon. How does that even stay on?

Is it weird that I'd be *more* embarrassed wearing her outfit than nothing?

I raise an eyebrow at her and toss the last of my third slice in my mouth.

"Brook... they've got her!"

"What?" I jump to my feet, grabbing her shoulders. "Mom?"

She starts crying and clamps on in a hug, sniffling into my shoulder. "Yeah."

My door swings in, revealing Jason. "Hey, I'm..." He stops short, staring at the two of us. "Missing out?"

I practically see his brain catch fire and blow out his ears as smoke. Laniah's supernaturally pretty in that red-eyed blonde innocent girl next door sort of way, and her outfit doesn't leave very much to the imagination. He stares at us. I think all the blood ran to his crotch, so his brain is starving for oxygen.

"What do you mean 'they got her?'" I ask. "What happened?"

Laniah leans back from the hug. "The ones who want war took your mother. I can't find her anywhere."

"Shit!" I spin toward Jason. "My mother's been kidnapped. I gotta go."

He snaps out of his horny fog and makes eye contact with me. "Damn... You're sure? Who's got her? Call the police?"

"Umm, no. They couldn't possibly help with this."

He runs over and puts an arm around me. Okay, he keeps glancing at Laniah, but I can't blame him. Her chest is like a bug-zapper for dudes. "Is this more angel/demon stuff?"

"Yeah," I say, shaking from a mixture of worry and anger.

Jason hugs me. Despite that he can't do a damn thing to help Mom, his warm hands on my back still somehow offer reassurance. "Anything I can do to help?"

"Yeah… don't freak out. And… maybe watch Ashley if she shows up. Not expecting her to, but she has a habit of walking in unannounced."

"Okay." He squeezes me tighter for a second, then lets go. "What's the plan?"

I rush to my bedroom and grab the chibi succubus amulet. Jason's staring mesmerized at Laniah when I walk back into the living room. He snaps out of it, turning his head to follow my stride to the front door.

"Umm… Brook? You're naked."

"Yeah. I know." I pat the amulet and the 'goth faerie' illusion of clothing appears. "Pretty sure clothing won't survive this."

Laniah hurries over to me. "Yeah. That's why I'm wearing this. It isn't uncomfortable under armor."

I pull the door open and head out. "Not sure that's enough material to even count as 'wearing' something."

She emits a nervous laugh. "It's an illusion, too."

"Bye," calls Jason from the door. "Be careful!"

They have Mom. Careful is the last thing on my mind. I barge into the stairwell and head for the roof.

"Please tell me your armor isn't like a metal bikini."

She laughs. "Where did you get that from? Of course not."

"Blame Hollywood."

"Look, I'm really sorry. I don't know how they got her. I was watching her the whole time and she just disappeared."

"If you were watching her, what did you see happen?" I shove the door out of my way, take three steps across the roof, and leap into the air.

Laniah, her long feathery wings aglow with golden light, pulls up alongside me. "I wasn't literally watching her with my eyes. More like I focused on her life presence. If any Elestari or Shaar'Nath went near her, I would've sensed them coming. But they didn't."

Maybe I'm becoming too casual with the flying thing, since it doesn't take me much effort at all to point myself toward Allentown by sight alone. Though it appears like I have wings phasing through a ghostly, frilly black goth dress, the wind blowing down my front is a constant reminder the fabric isn't real. Being cold only makes me angrier. I channel that anger and discomfort into wrath. Prison movies always mention that cliché of kicking someone's ass on day one. Maybe it's about time I rip some fuckin' heads off so these jackasses leave me the hell alone.

"So, what… Mom just disappeared? Where is she? Can't you like… tell?"

Laniah makes this face like a little girl who doesn't want to admit she broke something.

"What?"

She sighs. "We can sense the presence of a specific human anywhere in the Armistice. Sometimes, they become lost in the noise if they go somewhere with a lot of other people. Our kind are much easier to locate. But… Umm…"

"Mom's no longer in the Armistice."

"Yeah." She bites her lip. "I'm *really* sorry. I have no idea how they did it. She left her house for about an hour, and soon after she came back—she went poof. Never sensed any Elestari or Shaar'Nath near her."

"Any idea where she went or why?"

"No."

I reach for my cell phone, but grab my bare hip. Grr. I pour on as much speed as I can. Natalie did a good job with the illusion, but it's pretty obvious that they're fake when I'm flying about 300 miles an hour and the fabric is barely reacting to the wind.

Minutes later, Allentown comes into view below. I angle toward Mom's neighborhood.

"I'm not sensing anyone at the house."

Tears leak out the corners of my eyes. "There's gotta be something there. Some clue or message they want me to find."

"Sorry."

I glance over at her. "Stop apologizing and help me kick someone's ass."

# 19

## MAGICAL TAMPERING

I dive in for a landing in Mom's backyard, startling the hell out of two young boys.

Laniah lands beside me, and they go from startled to star struck.

Neither are old enough to truly appreciate her skimpy outfit, so it's gotta be the wings, or maybe 'seeing an angel.' I want to say the slightly taller one is Miguel… Mom is friends with his mother.

"Hello, boys," says Laniah, smiling at them. She raises her hand toward them and a wash of golden light dances around their eyes.

The kids stare into space, catatonic.

Laniah's wings go from feathery to pure energy, then shrink into her back. Taking the cue, I put mine away as well.

She looks at me. "They won't remember seeing us."

"Why are they in my mother's backyard? Wait. Why am I asking you that…? I'm the psychic." I stare at the boys long enough to figure out they came in chasing a soccer ball. "Okay. Nothing to worry about."

Leaving the kids staring into space, I head to the back door of Mom's place. Since I didn't bring my keys, I resort to my old tactic of breaking and entering by using telekinesis to move the latch.

I reflexively call out, "Mom?" as I go inside, then clench my fists in anger.

Laniah doesn't tease me for that, which I'm grateful for. Honestly, I'm kinda shocked she's so upset about the situation. Elestari are even more prone to thinking of humans as worthless ants than Shaar'Nath. But I guess even 'angels' have their free spirits and tree huggers. Maybe to her, humans are like some cute little helpless critters that she feels the need to 'save,' sorta like sea turtles... or in some cases, manatees.

Nothing initially looks unusual, so I run out the front door. Her car's parked on the street nearby, trunk open, two grocery bags dropped on the porch. Well, that explains where she went.

"It appears someone or something grabbed her right off the porch," says Laniah, eyeing the bags.

I'm so wound up, pissed off, and worried, my brain short circuits and puts me on autopilot. I pounce on the bags and pick them up. Mom wouldn't want to let her food go bad. A few back and forth trips to the car later, I find myself standing in the kitchen, staring at a table full of shopping bags. Nervous energy keeps me going, and I pack away all the frozen or refrigerated stuff while yelling mentally at myself for wasting time.

Laniah stands back watching me with a note of confusion.

"Sorry... I'm freaking out and it's just a reflex. I can't let food spoil. Had it kinda crappy growing up."

Once anything that needs cold is safe, I grab the wall phone and call Mom's number. Hey, stranger things have worked.

"We're sorry. The cellular subscriber you have dialed is no longer within our coverage area," says a recorded voice.

"Shit!" I hang the phone up hard.

Laniah puts a hand on my shoulder. "What's wrong?"

"Tried to call her. Out of coverage area."

"She's no longer on this plane."

"Oh... right. You said that already. I'm losing it. Probably for the best. Inter-dimensional roaming charges would suck."

"What?" asks Laniah.

"Forget it."

I run from room to room touching any object that I think isn't exactly where it ought to be. The only psychic hit I get is from one of her crystal owls, and it's only a view of Mom cleaning it. Wow, she must really love those things if she left an imprint.

Frustrated, I head back downstairs and go out the front door. There has to be something here, and I'm just not sensing it. I'm clearly too scatterbrained with worry to focus. Deep breaths. They're not going to hurt her. If they wanted to do that, they wouldn't have taken her anywhere. Mom's okay, I just need to collect myself.

A glimmer of supernatural energy comes from the doorjamb. Okay... that's something. I touch the wood and try to open myself to whatever psychic imprint might be there, but draw a blank. Grr.

At my growling, Laniah walks up to the door, still inside the house. "What?"

"There's something here, but I can't read it."

She examines the door.

While she's doing that, my frustration level boils over. I hate feeling like I'm in over my head, but Mom shouldn't suffer for my pride. "Dad!?"

"Magic was used here. Strong magic," says Laniah.

My father walks up beside me on the left without fanfare—or a suggestively shaped cloud of energy. "You've got an interesting friend."

Laniah freezes, then shifts her gaze from the top of the doorway to Dad. "Baal'nethiel."

"What?" I ask, glancing back and forth between them. "You two know each other?"

"Only in the sense that she's one of *them*," says Dad.

With a silvery shimmer, a stunningly beautiful set of silvery metal armor appears on Laniah, covering everything but her head and wings—and even they have a strip of segmented armor along the top edge.

Oh, shit. This is going to escalate, isn't it?

I step in front of him, feeling a little too much like I'm trying to keep my father from attacking an 'undesirable boyfriend.' Not that I've ever experienced that, but I've seen movies. "Dad, calm down. Laniah's on our side."

"Which side is that?" he asks. "And I am calm."

"The not-destroying-the-world side." It finally hits me that she called him Baal'nethiel. I peer over my shoulder at her. "How did you know his name?"

She takes a half step back into the house, her hand on a sword at her belt. "Most of us recognize the Harvester."

Dad offers a disarming smile. "While I appreciate the compliment, I am not who you think I am. The one you know as the Harvester is my father. I am nowhere near old enough to have participated in the war."

"Your kind deceive with ease," says Laniah.

"And your kind think humans are a half step up from pond algae." I smirk at her. "*You* don't… so maybe cut my old man some slack?"

"I'm not old." Dad folds his arms.

Laniah lowers her hand from her blade, but her posture remains tense and defensive. "You look so much like him."

"Who is this Harvester dude anyway?" I ask.

"A general who slaughtered my people in great numbers and nearly brought about our extinction." Laniah bows her head.

Dad takes a step toward her, easing me aside. "Child, you've only heard one side of that story. Not that I'm surprised. My father was a general, yes. He led many successful campaigns, yes. At the time he rose to prominence, the Elestari had a clear advantage. My people are… chaotic, to put it bluntly. We are just as likely to lay around drinking or fornicating as pick up a weapon and fight for our survival. Elestari are ordered and disciplined. My father managed to… what is the phrase the humans like so much? 'Herd cats?' He organized a large group to fend off several waves of attacks before leading a charge across Silvermist into Aesinor."

"He massacred thousands," yells Laniah. "Far more than any other Shaar'Nath."

"No worse than any of your war leaders. Your people hate him because he stole victory from their fingertips. Without his leadership, my kind would have been annihilated."

"He nearly exterminated us!"

Dad flashes his 'trust me' smile. "Our people nearly exterminated each other. That is why the Armistice was made. Continued war would have resulted in the destruction of both sides. Whether you believe me or not is irrelevant, but he much prefers the Armistice to remain as well. One does not need to enjoy killing to be proficient at it."

"Guys..." I hold my hands out like I'm stopping traffic in two directions. "Mom is missing. Can we maybe rain check the history lesson?"

"What?" Dad blinks at me. "Reya?"

"The warmongers think they can kidnap her and use her somehow to threaten me into destroying the armistice."

He stares.

"Yeah. I know. It's the dumbest thing I've ever heard. But that didn't stop them from doing it." I bite my lip. "Something magic happened here. Can you find her?"

Laniah relaxes enough to resume running a hand over the doorjamb. "This wooden frame recently contained a portal."

Dad steps past me to the door. Despite his harmless grey suit and lack of weapons, Laniah tenses again. "The magic activated when the door opened, drawing Reya in before collapsing."

"A teleport trap," says Laniah.

"Most likely, they sent her to one of the Pillars of Creation." Dad picks at the doorjamb. "An interesting tactic. Neither I, nor any full-blood Shaar'Nath or Elestari can go there."

"Humans can?" I ask.

"Yes, though they cannot harm the pillar, and I suspect they would likely find it unpleasant to be there." Dad looks off to the side, seeming worried for the first time since I've known him.

"Are you being sarcastic?" I ask. "Does 'unpleasant' mean she's going to die?"

Laniah sighs at the wall. "I can't reopen this, but I might be able to figure out where it went."

"Okay." I nod. "I have to go after her."

Dad puts a hand on my shoulder, blinks, then pats down my arm before gripping my side.

"Illusion." I tap the amulet. "Got tired of being stranded bare-assed."

"But you're still not wearing anything." He chuckles.

"I never cared about *being* naked. It's being *seen* that causes problems. And can we please focus on Mom here?"

"It isn't a good idea for you to go after her." Dad looks down again. "If you travel there, our allies will think you're trying to destroy the world."

I snarl again, the deep bear-like sound startling a dog across the street into barking. "I can't leave Mom there. You'll just have to convince them that I'm only going there to get her back. And…" I take a step closer, jabbing my finger into his chest. "Fuckin' tell the other idiots that this is not gonna work. If I do what they want, everyone dies anyway. Exploiting those I care about is pointless."

Laniah stands in the doorway bracing her hands on both sides, eyes closed, whispering some manner of chant in a language I can't follow.

Dad makes a face like he's trying to come up with something to say that'll talk me out of going… or maybe he's practicing whatever speech he's going to lay on the pro-Armistice side so they don't lose their shit when I travel to the pillar.

Yeah, he's got a point. Me even going there has bad idea written all over it… in red Sharpie.

"Fuck!" I shout.

Laniah jumps.

"Something wrong?" asks Dad. "Err, more wrong than already?"

"Argh!" I pace around the porch, grabbing my hair. "You told me that it takes magic to even go in there. I don't have magic."

Dad's brow knits. "I…" He closes his mouth, puts on an unreadable expression for a few seconds, then bursts into laughter.

Laniah raises an eyebrow at him. "What part of anything that's going on now is funny?"

I indicate her with my thumb. "What she said."

He scoops me off my feet and spins around a few times, still laughing. Okay, this is a little awkward... being held by my father when I have nothing but illusions on. It doesn't seem to bother him, but I guess he didn't grow up surrounded by human 'morals.' There's not a scrap of anything but parental affection and amusement radiating from him, so I push aside the oddity of it.

"This is not the reaction I was expecting," I say.

Dad puts me back on my feet, grinning. "They're fools. The ones who set this whole thing in motion forgot to take that into account. You *can't* destroy the world because you have no way into the pillars' dimensional chamber."

"Okay. Normally, I'd be like, yay, cool—but Mom." I freeze at a sudden realization. "Son of a bitch!"

"What?" asks Laniah and Dad at the same time.

"Now it makes sense." I flail my arms. "That's what Melisandre wanted with Eaves. Mages."

"Who is Eaves?" asks Laniah.

"A mage. He's tomato sauce now, but he was talking via orb with Melisandre. I couldn't figure out what the Elestari would want from human mages, but now it makes sense. I don't have the magical abilities to open a way into that place, so he needed a human to compensate for that. The place is shielded against magic from Elestari, right?"

Laniah nods.

Dad frowns. "Simple enough to fix that. We'll cull the humans who work with them."

"You can't just kill them all! They're harmless and innocent," says Laniah, sounding oh so much like a PETA protestor.

Heh, she should start EETH. Elestari for the Ethical Treatment of Humans.

"People aren't quite as innocent as lab rabbits, but... yeah I gotta go with her here. Sorry, Dad. Exterminating any human mage you think might be conspiring with Melisandre is a bit over the top."

"The other side of the portal they opened here landed in Antarctica." Laniah cringes. "It's possible that your mother is already... well, it's really cold there."

I step to the edge of the porch and pop my wings. "No time to waste... unless you can somehow like teleport us there."

"The polar continents are warded." Laniah shakes her head. "Humans can use apportation magic to go there, but our kind cannot."

"Wait." I whirl around, nearly slapping Dad in the face with a wing. "How did the Earth wind up so important to the Armistice when it's all of the known universe in this dimension?"

"In and of itself, the Earth isn't significant," says Dad. "This is merely where humans happened to come into being. A few thousand years ago, the first group of those who wished to return to war established a gateway to the Pillar of Eternity—that's the one located inside the Armistice—here so that humans... or demi-humans like you could go there more easily."

Laniah throws a ball of golden light past me that strikes a pair of college-age guys on the sidewalk who'd been staring at the goth faerie and a woman in silver medieval armor. "Now, they think we're going to a cosplay convention."

I really ought to put my wings away, but I don't.

"The warmongers grew tired of waiting for humans to invent the technological or arcane means necessary to travel to the center of the universe." Laniah traces a doorway in the air. "So they made a portal there. The pacifists found out about it and enacted a ward."

"You have heard of the Big Bang Theory?" asks Dad.

"The sitcom or the physics thing?" I ask.

"Sitcom?" Dad raises an eyebrow.

"Never mind. Yeah. Some like point of origin where the whole universe blew up from?"

He nods at me. "Exactly. That is the location of the Pillar of Eternity. It is the focal point from which the Armistice came into being."

"There's no damn way anything technological could get there. Humans barely made it to the Moon before giving up on space. And that wasn't much more than an airtight metal box with teleportation enchantments. Some people still don't even think they really went up there." I twitch my wings, itching to get moving. "We have to fly then. Mom's in Antarctica with nothing but street clothes. She doesn't have much time."

"By the time you flew there, she'd already be gone." Dad bows his head.

"No, she won't." I grab him and shake. "Laniah said she's not in this plane anymore. Roaming charges, remember?"

Dad gives me a look as if I'd randomly switched to Russian. "What?"

"She's not in Antarctica. She might've gone there, but she isn't there anymore. Come on." Again, I run to the edge of the porch.

"She traversed the portal to the Pillar." Laniah stares into space. "It's the only explanation. You'll need to go through that portal as well to find her."

"Wait." Dad points at her. "This is starting to sound a bit too convenient. How do we know you aren't posing as her friend, trying to trick her? Now, you're encouraging her to enter the portal into the Pillar of Eternity, which is precisely the worst possible place for her to go."

"I give you my word, my motives are pure." Laniah bows her head. "I promised to leave this one alone after what happened last time, but... she needs a friend."

"Wait." I whirl again—whacking Laniah in the face with my right wing—"What do you mean 'this one?' What happened last time?"

She backs up, sputtering, then playfully swats at me. "Watch where you stick those. And I'm talking about Joan of Arc. She, umm... kinda went a little nuts. I tried to talk her out of destroying the universe. Well, the warmongers convinced her the pillars were demonic creations responsible for all the world's suffering. She asked me for help with some political stuff, and became totally sidetracked with that for a while. It kept her mind off destroying the pillars so I helped her out with that mess... but she thought she was visited by angels and went a little crazy."

"Oops," I deadpan.

Dad chuckles. "She's *still* pissed off."

Laniah frowns. "She won't talk to me. Like it's my fault. I never *tried* to trick her. She saw me and thought 'angel.' It's like seeing an eagle and calling it a pigeon. Just because I have wings... Every human-shaped being with wings isn't an angel."

"I'm a human-shaped being with wings." I flutter them.

"Argh! You know what I mean. The girl had issues." Laniah puts her hands on her hips and pouts. "And I'm really sad that she's so angry with me."

I grab Laniah by the wrist and drag her to the porch edge. "We're going to Antarctica. You've got magic. You can open the door for me."

"This is going to be bad." Dad stands there in silence for a few seconds before huge, leathery wings unfurl from his back. "But... I trust you."

"You don't need to drag me around like a child," says Laniah. "Let's go before I have to erase anyone else's memory."

With that, I leap into the air, Laniah and my father behind me in a vee.

Oh great, like I know where I'm going.

How hard could Antarctica possibly be to find?

# 20

# THE GATEWAY

Sometimes, being impulsive can get me in trouble.

It's landed me in police custody quite a few times, but acting without giving it any serious thought beforehand has never really threatened my life. Flying on a whim from Philly to Antarctica on the other hand isn't one of my brightest moments. Once we climb high enough, I shift to my armored form, both to spare my eyes and because it's warmer than wearing illusions.

We're somewhere over... Alabama I think, when Dad mentions it will take us something like thirty hours to get there. Whoops.

"Not that long." Laniah waves us closer and takes the lead, holding both our hands.

Her wings take on an even brighter golden radiance, almost becoming pure energy instead of feathers. Strong tingles wash over me, and Dad emits an odd noise like someone poured warm pudding into his pants.

The ground going by under us picks up speed. I let out a yell of pain at a sensation like a giant trying to pluck my wings.

"Tuck them in a little," yells Laniah.

I glance over and notice how she's folded hers in close, the bend at the joint the farthest-forward part. She kinda looks like a military combat jet with the back-swept wings. Alas, my wings are a little bulkier, but I do my best to mimic the position, as does Dad. The relief from pain is immediate, and with the reduced drag, we go slightly faster. At this speed, air friction on my tail blade feels like I've got an annoying child tugging on it.

The wind in my face makes talking more painful than annoying, so I don't bother asking how fast we're going. This is well beyond any speed I can reach on my own. Since no loud bangs happened, I'm pretty sure we haven't exceeded the speed of sound.

Laniah also seems to have an idea of where to go, which I don't. So, I'm fine letting her take the lead of our formation. Well, so much for my weekend of doing nothing. An unplanned trip to the bottom of the Earth wasn't anywhere near even remotely on my list of 'things that might happen.' It wouldn't have even entered my thoughts as a joke.

We zoom over the rest of the United States, then Mexico. I think a couple military jets try to come after us, but we're too small and fast for them to find by the time they start trying to figure out what buzzed over them. Three dragons take notice of us once we're out over open ocean, though they have better things to do than pester us. Pretty sure they can sense what we are—or at least what Dad and Laniah are—and have no interest. That does distract me for a little while with idle wonderings about the relative power levels of various magical creatures and us. On one hand, considering the Elestari and Shaar'Nath created this entire dimension, I assume we're higher up on the food chain so to speak. But, then again, humans made cars and cars kill plenty of people.

Hours drag by without much noticeable change in daylight. Actually, it is getting darker but damn gradually. We've got to be flying west across time zones as much as we're going south.

After quite a long time—and one rather awkward midair bathroom break—the endless ocean finally reveals an enormous mass of whiteness up ahead. The magical energy that Laniah had been radiating for most of our trip fades. We all start to drop at the same time until she flares her wings out to full length. I do the same, as does

Dad, and we cruise in at a speed closer to the mere 350 miles per hour or so I'm used to flying at when I'm 'sprinting.'

"Stupid question. What time is it?" I yell.

"No idea." Laniah does her best to shrug while holding our hands.

Dad glances over at her. "We had to be doing almost seven hundred miles per hour."

She laughs. "Something like that. No idea. I never paid attention to humans' measurements."

"Holy shit you guys can fly fast." I gawk.

"Magic. The same way humans use spells to make themselves stronger or tougher. Holding it that long is tiring. I'm about ready to sleep."

"It's about twelve or thirteen hours since we left," says Dad.

Shit. I hope my mother's not frozen. "Is Mom still out of the plane?"

"Yes," says Laniah. "I can't sense her at all."

"Umm." I bite my lip. "Could that mean she's…"

Laniah squeezes my hand. "No. I would've felt her life depart if that happened."

I take a deep breath of icy air. It hurts, but hearing her say Mom's definitely alive makes it feel like I'm inhaling hope. She veers to the right and enters a slight dive. Pure white nothingness stretches out ahead of us, expanding until the dark blue of seawater below us gives way to ice. I catch sight of a collection of small buildings off to the left, some kind of research station. We avoid it, heading deeper into the continent.

"Let me guess, it's at the South Pole."

Laniah laughs. "No… there are people there. The portal stands on a mountainside that's nearly impossible to reach by land."

"Another stupid question. Why aren't my boobs freezing off?"

"Magic," says Laniah. "This place is cold enough to freeze me, too. At least you guys can bask in fire. We can't take too much heat *or* too much cold."

"Perhaps I misjudged your friend." Dad smiles at me. "She is proving quite helpful."

Laniah steers us left a bit, heading for a mountain range. "It makes sense why they chose you to be her father. They likely assumed you would make her warlike."

"The Harvester's greatest strength isn't his bloodlust, but his ability to motivate others. He's actually fairly lazy." Dad laughs.

"I can confirm that." I hold up a finger. "If lazy is an inheritable trait, I got it."

We glide in for a landing on the windy side of a mountain where the constant gale has kept loose snow from accumulating. Ahead, the peaks converge forming a short canyon that ends at an alcove beneath a rocky overhang. Two stone columns hint at the outline of a large doorway, though they aren't obviously unnatural. They don't look particularly natural either. Humans finding this would probably start wondering if aliens exist… or if this is some manner of temple to the Old Gods.

I take a step closer, but my heel shoots out from under me and I land in a full splits.

Dad cringes.

Not wanting to look any more graceless, I 'fly' back to my feet and dig my toe claws into the ice. We trudge onward, entering the canyon, mercifully escaping the constant wind. Sixty feet or so later, we stop near the alcove at the end. Footprints in the snow, and another Supremo Food Market bag on the ground, tell me Mom was here. I pick up an orange, hard enough to break a window with, then drop it. Her tracks appear out of thin air five feet away from the blank rock wall.

"She must've landed here and either tripped through the next portal or been pushed," I say.

"Without my magic on you keeping you warm, you'd totally understand why she might've jumped into the portal on her own." Laniah shivers.

"Guess it's warm inside?" I ask.

"Temperate, I imagine." Dad shrugs. "I've never been there."

"Smartass."

Laniah glances at me. "What? How's he being a smartass?"

"Full bloods *can't* go there, right?" I ask.

"Oh." She nods. "Duh. Okay, hang on. I can open this gate." Laniah starts to raise her arms, but hesitates, glancing at me. "You promise you won't break the world?"

"Absolutely swear I won't." I fold my arms. "I still have a season and a half of *Dead Like Me* to watch. I can't let the universe end at least until I finish it."

Dad raises an eyebrow. "You've watched it dozens of times already."

"That's beside the point. My weekend of nothing has been interrupted by a kidnapping. About the only thing so far going to plan is my not having to put on pants. I didn't want to leave my house at all. Now I'm in Antarctica."

Laniah closes her eyes. Blue light forms around her fingertips.

An array of shimmering silver columns and energy clouds appears in front and on either side of us, then fades, revealing a group of forty or so Elestari and Shaar'Nath.

I pivot toward Dad and Laniah, one arm extended out toward the group. "How the fuck did they just teleport here? I thought you said you couldn't do that?"

Laniah does a spot on impression of a clueless blonde who lost her Beemer in a parking lot.

"I believe it is because you are here," says Dad. "A being who is both capable of entering the Pillar as well as damaging it."

Most of the group approaches, except for two Elestari and a Shaar'Nath with grey armor who fall back to stand guard at the stone columns. The remaining Elestari draw silver swords and approach us along with the Shaar'Nath who—except for one giant dude with a polearm—have only their claws.

"Stop!" I shout. "Hang on a minute."

"You assured us that you had no intention of disrupting the Armistice," says a rather haughty sounding Elestari my age with perfect blond hair and emerald eyes, pointing his sword at me. "Clearly, you lied."

I lock stares with Daniel Graf... or Ezriel, the bartender from

Niflheim, also the prig who's been following me all over the place for weeks. "No, I didn't."

"Yet here you are." Ezriel lifts his head in a contemptuous sneer.

"Look, blondie, I'm here because the morons who want the Armistice to fall have abducted my mother and thrown her through the portal. I'm not going to let her starve to death in there. Didn't come here to destroy the pillar. All I want to do is bring my mother home."

Ezriel steps closer. "Even if I believe that—touching story by the way—you are speaking of a mere human. They are not worth the potential risk."

The rest of the group murmurs, sounding mostly in agreement with him.

"That's my *mother!*" I roar, leaping into a punch.

His silvery blade flies up, meeting my fist with a near-blinding flash of light and a *clang* that echoes over the canyon. Ezriel whirls with the grace of a ballet dancer and thrusts his blade at my back faster than I can move out of the way. Laniah darts in and swats his attack aside, giving me the chance to jump back.

"Traitor," he hisses, before swinging at her.

Their swords clash with sparks, the two 'angels' staring at each other over the X of steel crossed between them. Much to my surprise, she pushes him back despite being smaller.

"Brooklyn is no threat to the Armistice," roars Dad.

Whoa. It didn't really hit me while we flew all damn day long, but he's huge without his human disguise on. Gotta be eleven feet tall, his armor as white as mine. The blade at the end of his tail looks more like a damn broadsword than a spike. His presence coupled with the depth of his voice and its volume makes *me* cringe back like a scolded kid.

The Shaar'Nath among the group hesitate, though the other Elestari show no such restraint. Laniah and Ezriel continue trading swipes as another ten or so gold-winged assholes swarm after me. I'm so damn pissed off at Mom being kidnapped, the cold, and everyone being such unreasonable jackasses, I lose the ability to give a shit.

I dive at the first Elestari to come near me, blasting her with a telekinetic force wave that knocks her off balance enough for me to land a fist into her chin. A man runs at me from the right rear the instant my knuckles make contact with the woman, his sword poised to go for my throat. He doesn't see my tail coming, and staggers sideways with about eight inches stuck between his ribs. I grab the sword out of the hand of the woman I knocked flying and spin to face another guy, jumping back from his swing before chopping at him.

He teaches me pretty quick I have no idea how to swordfight... the stolen blade flying out of my fingers after three seconds. The dude gives me this disdainful 'you gotta be kidding' look.

"What? When exactly was I supposed to learn sword fighting?"

A constant *clang, clang, clang,* echoes from somewhere behind me, Ezriel and Laniah trading strikes as well as insults. He, and some of the other Elestari goad the Shaar'Nath for just standing there and not stopping the end of the Armistice, though they appear more afraid of my father than anything else.

The guy moves to attack me but I take his foot out with a telekinetic jab, simultaneously leaning back so his blade misses my face by a few inches. He recovers, and three more 'angels' rush over to hem me in.

"Baal'nethiel," rasps Laniah, "need a moment."

Four Elestari surround me, which leaves me no choice but to even the odds by going for kills. These idiots want the same thing I do, so I *was* trying to be nice, but... nice only goes so far. A woman at my rear left and the guy at my front right attack simultaneously. I leap to the left and forward, dodging his blade and half-tackling the woman next to him. A sword hits me in the chest, but the angle's too weak to penetrate my armor and it glances off. I spin to my right, throwing the woman I grabbed into the other woman before she can take my head off.

The Elestari crashes into her friend, accidentally impaling her, and they both tumble to the ground, sliding off on the ice.

Before I can spit out a sarcastic comment about running with sharp things, the second man raises his left arm at me, several concentric rings of yellow light appearing around his hand. Golden chains erupt from the ice, grabbing at my forearms. More wrap up around my legs, tying me to the ground. The ones on my arms drag me down to my knees.

With a cocky grin, the Elestari who thinks he's hot shit with the magic saunters up to me, points his sword at my neck, and rears back in preparation for a swing. I swipe my tail up and hack his left hand off at the wrist. The golden light explodes in a burst of dazzling sparks; the chains disintegrate. He staggers to the side, waving his arm, silver energy spewing out of the stump.

Somewhere behind me, Ezriel screams in anger, but the shout distorts like a speeding train going by. I spring back to my feet, claws bared and snarling at the bastard who chained me to the ground. A loud *whump* comes from the same direction Ezriel's scream went. The other male Elestari, plus two Shaar'Nath, charge at me. I run in the only open direction out of being surrounded and jump over the two women, the one on top in the middle of some kind of healing spell.

"Brooklyn!" shouts Laniah.

I instinctively twist toward her voice. She's standing in the midst of total chaos—Elestari swords and Shaar'Nath claws everywhere in a dazzling, beautiful spectacle of blue, silver, and white. Dad, a few paces from her, has the giant onyx polearm, its former owner headfirst in the ice wall next to Ezriel. It's like Mount Rushmore, only with asses. Laniah thrusts her empty left hand at me.

After that last guy, I jump up to avoid another set of chains, but a blunt force wave hits me full-on. The strike is somewhat more comfortable than walking in front of an inattentive bus driver. It knocks me spinning head over ass at what is no longer a bare rock wall but a huge curtain of white-blue energy.

A sword or two, as well as some claws, nip at my legs. I feel the strikes on my armor, but they don't hurt. I barely have time to realize she opened the gateway before I hit the energy curtain. The last sight burned into my brain before everything goes black is Laniah and my dad disappearing under a crowd of extraplanar morons trying to kill them.

# 21

# PILLAR OF ETERNITY

Calm weightlessness surrounds me.

All the roar of fighting and the howl of the wind above the canyon are gone. I can't even see my body, or move.

"What the f"—I land face down on grey stone hard enough to knock the air out of my chest—"uck." I groan. "Ow. That hurt."

My voice echoes.

When I lift my head away from the rock, I find myself sprawled on the floor of a huge cave, wings flopped to either side, my tail coiled around my left leg. I totally look (and feel) like I got hit by a bus and thrown to the side of the street.

With a grunt, I gather my legs under myself and stand. Behind me, the curtain of swirling blue energy stretches up to the height of a two-story building, give or take a couple feet. It's opaque, filled with energy, offering no view of the world beyond. On this side, the columns bordering the gateway are quite clearly the product of craftsmanship. The black marble one on the left is striated with glittery crimson. The one on the right is white with silver marbling. Hmm. Guess that represents each faction or something.

The cave walls look like glacial ice but the room isn't cold, so it's some manner of pale white stone. No sign of any footprints or tracks mark the ground, but I'd be more worried if my mother left footprints on a hard surface. She's gotta be in here. Opposite the gate, a large passage stretches into the distance. Something at the far end emits light, but it's so damn far away I can't make out what.

I glance down at my clawed, armored hands. If anyone had told me when I graduated from college that I would someday be standing in a place so far from Earth we haven't invented numbers to describe it yet, I'd have laughed at them.

Okay, maybe I'm lying. Numbers this big could exist... I just hate math.

"The center of the fucking universe... right. One small step for a man, or some bullshit, right?" I grumble. I'm neither a man nor really 'mankind.' There's a weird energy in this place. It definitely gives me the feeling I don't belong in here, like I'm a senior in high school with a mild interest in nursing who wandered into an operating room in the middle of brain surgery. This is an *epic* place for important creatures with important things to do... not my lazy ass.

I peer back at the gateway. Laniah and Dad are in deep shit that's getting deeper by the second. She punted me through the gate before we lost the chance to do so. Wow. I guess she does trust me... or, as Dad is worried about, she's hoping I blow things up.

Nah. I doubt it. My ability to read intention doesn't work on Elestari, but my gut feeling is that she's really that nice. Her reaction to me going in here to save my Mom is like how a human would react to a video of some random dude finding an orphan baby squirrel and bottle feeding it.

Right. Time limits and shit. Yay.

I jog forward into a run, then leap onto my wings. This cavern is big enough for a damn dragon. No sense walking. Stone rushes by me for about twenty seconds before I cruise out into a massive underground chamber. I stop short, hanging in midair over the ledge at the end of the cave where it deadfalls into a cliff.

Gleaming white stone walls form a maze stretching off to the horizon. It's pretty small, for someone who considers oh, New York City to be a 'hamlet.' This labyrinth would drive a minotaur insane.

Crap, I think a human would die of old age trying to navigate this mess, even if they made every single turn correctly.

Miles away, a huge column of whitish light stretches from the ground to the cave ceiling. Speaking of which, I get the sneaky suspicion this isn't a cave so much as maybe I'm inside a hollow planet or something. Caves don't usually have this much space.

Right... that energy column is giving off light and heat like a slightly scaled down version of the sun. Even from this distance, it's almost painfully hot to me... like Irish girl without sunscreen in the middle of August.

Yeah, yeah, I know... I'm one to talk about Irish girls. I make snowmen look tan.

So, that light either *is* or surrounds the Pillar of Eternity. Probably why it's giving off a really strong 'no touchie' vibe. And... I should stop staring at it. My mother's in here somewhere. The sooner I get out of here, the happier I'll be.

I glide forward, peering past the ledge at the tops of the maze walls about forty feet down. They're as wide as a city sidewalk, at least three stories tall, and pretty much featureless. Huh. I guess whoever made this place never imagined the destroyer would have wings. Why the hell would anyone deal with that bullshit twisty labyrinth when they could simply fly to the middle?

One path leads left from the ledge, circling around in a long loop to the ground level and 'official' entrance to the maze. I glide back and forth, searching the corridors from the air for any signs of Mom.

"Mom?" I shout.

Five seconds later, a feeble echo of a voice comes from a good distance ahead. Crap. It took us like fourteen hours to fly here. She's probably halfway to the damn pillar by now. I lean forward and pick up speed, heading toward her.

Out of nowhere, I get this sudden feeling of impending dread. I haven't felt like this since my mom nearly walked in on me touching myself. Nervous, I stop to a hover, rotating in place. I don't initially notice anything unusual until a shadow falls over me. Instinctively, I zoom to the left. I've seen enough Wile E. Coyote cartoons to understand a giant shadow means there's a big ass rock falling on me.

Said big ass rock passes by close enough for its furry hide to bump into me, and a loud *crack* like a medieval castle portcullis falling closed.

That's a metaphorical rock by the way. When I stop spinning from being sideswiped by a multiple-ton beast, I gawk in horror at a furry dragon-shaped creature with brilliant sky blue horns, matching teeth, and enormous leathery wings of dark indigo. The rest of it, except for patches around the eyes, is covered in silvery white fur. Okay, it can't decide if it wants to be a yeti or a dragon.

It occurs to me that the jarring crack I heard most likely came from its jaws narrowly missing me.

Shit… Well, okay, that's one reason someone would stay in the maze. This fat, fluffy thing can't fit between the walls.

The creature wheels around and charges at me again. I zip straight up, but it keeps right on me. Only a telekinetic shove at its head keeps me from going straight down its throat. I pivot to keep my wings clear as its jaws crash closed *way* too close for comfort. It wrenches its long serpentine neck toward me and tries again.

I feel like a damn moth trying to avoid a small dog with a serious case of 'nom the fluttery thing.' Three near-death-experiences later, I flip over backward and dive straight down. Gravity lends me speed enough to stay a few feet ahead of the dragon until I plunge down between two pale white walls. I nearly pull a wing muscle stopping myself before kissing the ground, then look up at the massive furry beast. Its head can't quite fit into the maze corridor, which is super claustrophobic… only a little wider than a standard doorway.

It lands above me like a cat that just swatted its toy under the stove.

"You're some kind of guardian, aren't you?"

The creature narrows its eye. Probably narrowed both of them, but I can only see one right now.

"Look, I get it. You're here to stop anyone from destroying the universe. That's cool. We're on the same team. I'm not going to destroy anything. I only want to find my mom."

It snorts.

Damn if it doesn't sound like a 'yeah right' reaction.

Okay, whatever. I just have to outrun this sucker. There's no reason for me to go anywhere near the middle of the chamber. I fly down the passageway, but the narrowness forces my wings pretty much straight back behind me. Good thing I stay airborne mostly by supernatural desire rather than aerodynamics.

A couple quick turns and—

*Whap.*

Okay. Ouch. Now I know what it feels like for a fly to hit a windshield. That third left turn only went four feet before another corner. A wheezy, almost silent laugh comes from above. Oh screw you, dragon-yeti-whatever the hell you are.

I let gravity peel me off the stone and fall flat on my back, staring up past thirty feet of wall at the furry annoyance. There's no way I'm going to find my mother if I stay down here. Every second I loiter increases the odds that Laniah and my dad get exiled back to other dimensions. It's not like they're risking their lives for Mom, just the next, oh four or five decades. At least, I think that's how long it would be before they can re-enter the Armistice after the disruption of being 'killed' here. It's also why the warmongers are so fixated on destroying my world. They want to go back to killing each other for keeps.

And seriously... how messed up is that? Some of the Shaar'Nath and Elestari are working together so they can kill each other. I thought kidnapping my mom for leverage was stupid, but wow. Like, if they manage to somehow force or trick me into doing it someday down the road, are these guys going to look at each other and say 'awesome, we did it. Thanks for all the help—now die!'?

Ugh. Dumbasses.

I drag myself to my feet and leap straight up, flying into the furry dragon's belly. I'm sure my fist doesn't bother it too much, but punching it makes me feel better. It jumps, no doubt more from surprise than pain, allowing me to skim around its fluffy posterior and dash across the maze.

"Mom?" I shout.

A distant reply pulls me to the left.

The dragon dives on me, biting a chunk out of the wall when I swerve out of the way. Unfortunately, it also gets my tail. I go from flying to being pulled through the air ass first. Worse, the damn thing doesn't even notice it sorta got me, and flies in frantic circles trying to find me. I roll over and plant my feet against the side of its head, grabbing my tail in both hands. The motion of its rapid turns keeps slamming me into its cheek—fortunately, it's pretty soft.

Finally, it screeches in frustration, which parts the fire-hydrant-sized teeth enough for my tail blade to slip free. I take advantage of its momentary confusion to fly straight up over its back and skim the length of its body. The creature's tail whips up, giving me a really awesome close up view of the tip. It slaps me like a field hockey ball straight up. I think that hurt so much I didn't even feel it. My brain blocked it out. A few small cracks crisscross my armored chestplate from the hit, and I'm too stunned to do much of anything but tumble in the air for a few seconds before I realize I'm not breathing anymore.

When I take a gasp of air, the pain hits, but it's not *too* bad. Numbnuts clawing my wing membrane hurt more than this. I reorient myself from falling to flying barely two seconds before the dragon's giant sky-blue mouth opens beneath me.

So this is what a worm on a hook feels like when a huge fish is coming for it from below. Sideways is probably my worst option. I need to move faster than this thing can react, so I do the exact opposite thing common sense says, and zoom *toward* it.

I pull up at the last possible moment, skimming over its nose and crashing into its face right between the eyes.

Oof.

Of course, bouncing off its skull hurts a whole lot less than those giant teeth would have. I flip over and cling to the top of its head, not too worried about using my claws to hold on. Even if I break skin, my little nails couldn't possibly hurt this beast.

Enraged, the dragon pulls into a power climb. Guess he doesn't like his new Brooklyn hat.

Oh, I see what he's doing... heading for the ceiling covered in long spiky needles. Maybe he'll knock himself senseless. I watch the approaching rock, releasing my grip three seconds before impact. Of course, my momentum still causes me to slap back-first into the ceiling, but I don't have six tons of dragon on top of me. Its huge body shears off a few dozen stone lances, which plummet down into the maze. A few have stuck into its neck and shoulder, though it doesn't seem terribly concerned... like a pit bull with a couple porcupine quills. Whatever pain they caused it has become my fault.

It swipes at me, but its hand is so big, none of its claws make contact. A padded leathery mitt launches me sideways. My wing membranes scream out from the strain of me trying to avoid crashing into more spikes. I dive seconds before the dragon snaps its jaws shut around me.

Fuck this. I need a second to catch my breath.

I make for the maze again as fast as I can fly straight down.

Screeching with rage, the giant fur-covered dragon chases me all the way to the white walls. A great *whump* shakes the air around me, and I barely manage to 'slam on the brakes' before smacking into the floor hard enough to go splat.

I still smack into the floor, but only give myself a mild concussion and probably a dislocated shoulder.

My slide stops with my horns touching the wall of a corner. Ow. Even covered in armor, boobs don't make for great landing gear. I lay there for a moment, with pretty much zero desire to move. I can live without Laniah or Dad around for a few decades. They'll come back eventually. Yeah, they'll totally understand if I take a quick nap.

"Okay, I get it. I'm breaking the rules and not running the maze... but"—I raise my voice to shouting—"I'm not here to destroy the stupid pillar!"

A blast of hot, wet air rolls over me along with a nasal whine that kinda reminds me of a dog that did something it shouldn't have. Oh, what now? I heave a groan and push myself over. It's rather awkward to roll around in this narrow passage with a fourteen-foot wingspan. I eventually get upright and twist around to look at the top of the walls.

The dragon is slumped upon the maze, its head wedged from its attempt to snap me up before I got away. It twists and pulls, but can't seem to dislodge its skull from the top of the walls. Oh, it'll probably pop loose eventually, but I've got a couple seconds' advantage.

I pluck a nine-foot-long rock spire from the ground a short distance down the passageway. If this thing didn't shatter on impact, it's probably strong enough to punch a hole into this guardian dragon's brain. When it sees me flying up with a giant impaling stalactite of doom, the dragon groans and struggles harder. Bits of rock flake away from the walls, but its skull remains trapped.

The creature goes completely still when I land upon its head and plant the spike tip between my feet. It tries to roll its eyes up to stare at me.

"Okay. I have a feeling you can understand me. You can, right?"

It appears confused for a moment, probably that I haven't just killed it. It rotates its trapped head in something akin to a nod, making me wave my arms for balance.

"Good. You are here to protect the pillar and stop someone like me from destroying it, right?"

Again, it nods.

"I don't want to kill you, because that will leave the pillar vulnerable. This place needs to stay protected." I heft the big stone lance away from its skull and chuck it back down into the maze, where it sticks like a dart. "There. *Now* will you believe that I'm not here to do harm? I know I *can* do something shitty to the pillar, but some morons kidnapped my mother. That's the only reason I'm here. I *want* the pillar to exist. I like this world. Will you please stop trying to eat me?"

It grunts in a confused, resigned tone.

"I'll take that as a yes." I walk down onto its snoot and turn to face its eyes. "Is there a human woman here?"

It nods, pointing with its tail to my left.

"Awesome. I swear I'm not going to go near the pillar. Just find that woman and leave. You can follow me if you want and make sure I don't go for the middle, okay?"

It nods again, emitting a frustrated—and somewhat sad—tone.

"Okay, okay. Fine. One sec." I dive off its snoot and recover the stone spike, then fly up to stand on the wall by where the widest part of its head is lodged. "Relax. I'm just going to help you get loose."

Three good stabs into the stone breaks off enough of a chunk that the enormous creature can pull itself free. It shakes its head and gives me a wary glance.

"Come on. I really want to go home. Where's the human?"

The dragon lurches into the air, heading in the direction it pointed earlier. I fly up alongside its head, high enough that I've got a good view down into the maze passages. My escort keeps himself positioned between me and the pillar, and doesn't quite seem to trust me completely, but that's fine. I probably wouldn't trust me either in his position. Or hers. Can't tell.

Maybe its. This thing is as old as the Armistice, so I doubt there's a mate involved... or even any other creatures of its kind.

A flash of motion at ground level draws my attention to Mom running like mad from a quartet of white-skinned pod-bodied creatures that resemble goblins. They're only about waist high, but they've got claws that my mother's T-shirt and jeans won't protect against.

I swoop down and land a short distance ahead of her on top of the wall. I've had enough of the damn narrow passageway. She lets out a scream when I telekinetically drag her off her feet. One of the goblins gets a hold of her ankle, clinging as Mom floats up and out of the maze. As soon as they're close enough, I grab her and spear my tail blade into the goblin's face. The little bastard disintegrates into a blast of silvery light.

My mother takes one look at my fully shifted self and starts to scream, but stops before making a sound. "Brook? Is that you?"

"Yeah."

She cranes her neck to make eye contact. "I don't remember you being that tall. You should play basketball."

"Mom. You're in shock." I grasp her shoulders. And wow, it's weird looking down at my mother like she's the height of a tween.

"No I'm not. I was just running away from some demons. Something happened with the door at the house and everything got so cold and windy. I think it was a portal."

"I'll explain later. We need to get out of here."

Mom fusses at the crack in my chest plate. "Oh, you're hurt. What happened to you, sweetie?"

"Slight misunderstanding with an ancient dimensional guardian. Speaking of which, I made a deal with said guardian. We need to leave now while it still believes I'm not going to destroy the world."

Mom blinks. "That's ridiculous. Who would ever believe my sweet little girl would destroy the world?"

If I had eyebrows at the moment, I'd flatten them. Probably the same people who'd believe this 'sweet little girl' spray painted penises all over the chief of police's car.

"Come on." I scoop her up in my arms, stretch my wings, and flap into the air, heading for the maze.

The dragon follows close behind, still staring at me.

Later, pal. Hope I never see you again… no offense.

# 22

## A COLD RECEPTION

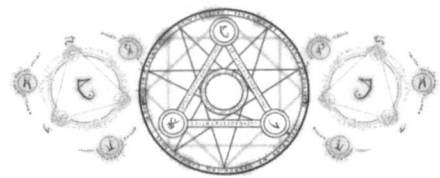

When we approach the large cave passage out of the maze chamber, the dragon stops to a hover, watching us.

I glide into land on the ledge and set Mom down on her feet. She peers over the side at the maze, then backs up before she falls.

"Oh, flying up was so much easier... I never thought I'd get out of that maze."

"Why did you go down there in the first place?"

She points at a waist-high hole in the wall near the cave leading out. "Those little demons came after me. Feels like I've been hiding or running away from them for a whole day."

"Yeah, about fifteen hours. Are you hurt?"

"Tired and cold, but no. At least it's warm in here." She fusses over me, picking at the occasional crack in my plating. "Oh, Brook... you've been in a fight, haven't you?"

"Yeah. Little misunderstanding outside."

"Oh, no... the groceries!"

I smile. "They're fine. I put them away for you."

She blinks. "What? How?"

"Long story. A friend of mine had sorta been keeping an eye on you, and she noticed you disappeared. So I went to your place."

"I'm sorry, Brooklyn. I should've believed you when you tried to warn me, but I don't think it would've mattered. The door… it just pulled me in."

"It's all right. C'mon. We're still not out of here."

Again, I scoop her up since I'd rather fly the half-mile to the gateway than walk. I don't go too fast with her in my arms, but we still reach the exit in under a minute.

"Oh, that's pretty," says Mom.

"It's going to be cold out there." I stop within a few feet of the wavering energy curtain. "Laniah has magic that will keep you warm."

"All right."

"Brace yourself… it's going to be damn cold for a little bit."

"Just go already. I'm not going to pull a coat out of thin air."

I try to steel myself as much as possible for the cold, and dash forward.

Hitting the gateway feels like I flew into a standing block of grape jelly. The weird squishy feeling goes away after a few seconds, leaving us floating in blank nothingness. I can't move or talk for the moment it takes us to traverse the non-space inside the magical conduit. Eventually, we pop out in Antarctica again.

I land on my feet near the two plain stone pillars. The gateway collapses behind us, leaving the wall blank. Not far in front of us, the melee continues raging, a chaotic mess of flashing blades, tails, and wings.

"Stop!" I shout, as loud as possible.

As if time itself ground to a halt, the entire battle scene freezes. Nothing moves except for thirty or so heads angling toward me. I spot Laniah near the center of it, held from behind by a Shaar'Nath pinning her arms up while an Elestari has a blade inches from her heart.

I can't help myself and telekinetically shove that guy away from her. He spills over on his back, sliding on the ice with his legs in the air.

Holy shit that was close.

"Stop fighting!" I scream. "I'm back and the world is still here, okay? Do you believe me now?"

Mom curls up in my arms, shivering, not even trying to speak.

"You're all a bunch of idiots! We're on the same team. I don't want to destroy the world. What is it going to take to convince you of that?"

Dad shoves an Elestari aside and stands up from under a pile of three more Shaar'Nath. He's covered in cuts and scratches, and one of his horns is half gone. Oddly, he looks thrilled, as if he'd had the time of his life. "If you going in there and coming out with the world still intact doesn't do it, I don't think anything will."

"Maybe she couldn't figure out how to break it?" asks an Elestari man.

I sigh. "There are others on both sides who want war and they are trying to make it happen. All of you are trying to kill me because you want to preserve the Armistice. *I* want to preserve the Armistice, too. I don't need *both* sides coming after me. Why don't you anti-war fuckers maybe try *helping* me? Why is everyone so insistent on stuffing their heads up their asses?"

Laniah grunts and jerks her arms away from the two men holding her. She unwraps a Shaar'Nath tail from her waist and hurries over, chanting in that indecipherable melodic language. Golden light surrounds her right hand and also appears over Mom, who stops shivering.

"Oh, my God," wheezes Mom. "It's s-s-so cold."

Laniah casts another spell on my mother, which I imagine heals frostbite. "Mrs. Amari... please forgive me. I should've protected you much better than I did. I feared showing myself to you might have been unwise."

Mom looks at her in awe. "You're going to tell me she's not an angel, aren't you, Brook?"

"Only if you call her one. She isn't. I have wings, but I'm not a bird."

"All right. Well, just because *you* aren't an angel doesn't convince me they don't exist."

Laniah's smile goes somewhat fake for a second. Shaking her head, she looks back toward the battle and holds out her hand. With a puff of snow, a silvery sword flies up into the air and races over into her grip. She slides it back into the scabbard on her belt.

A highly annoyed Daniel Graf—aka Ezriel—walks up to us.

"Oh, darn. You survived." I smirk.

He narrows his eyes.

"Look, I don't really want any of you to be hurt, but you gotta admit, you're a bit of a pompous asshat."

Mom stares at him, eyes widening, mouth hanging open.

"Oh, no. No. No. No. No." I shake my head. "My mother is not crushing on *this* guy."

"He's just so handsome," says Mom in a dreamy voice. "I'm not crushing on him."

"Mom, you forget I can feel people's intent." I sigh. "Really?"

"Compulsion." Dad walks over. "He's giving off a control aura to influence humans."

Mom abruptly stops gawking at him.

Ezriel gazes up at the skies as if asking for help from on high. "While some of us do believe you sincerely harbor no desire to destroy the Armistice, we fear you may be compelled or manipulated to do so."

Since she's no longer at risk of freezing, I set Mom down beside me, then fold my arms at the prick. "Will you guys at least wait for me to *be* compelled before you try cutting my head off? Hey, if I have to die to stop the universe from ending, whatever. But at least give me a damn chance."

Murmurs of conversation pass over the group. It's hard to tell how many—or if any—died since there's easily three times as many as were here when Laniah punted me through the portal. Guess reinforcements kept showing up. One by one, they start disappearing. Silver shimmers for the Elestari and crimson-black clouds of magical light for the Shaar'Nath.

Ezriel slides his sword back in the scabbard. "We will continue to watch you." He turns away with an oh-so-humble toss of his head that throws his hair over his shoulder, and walks over to rejoin the disappearing crowd.

"Hey," I whisper, "how about helping keep those other morons who you're so afraid will compel me *away* from me instead of making it all my fault?"

None of them say a word, though a few glance my way with expressions that verge on apologetic. Ugh. 'Gee, sorry we almost slaughtered you for no reason.' Jackasses.

Once the last of them have disappeared, I sigh at the barren white nothingness. "Are Shaar'Nath and Elestari *all* idiots?"

Laniah grins. "Weak impulse control runs on both sides."

"Okay." I face her and Dad. "How are we going to get Mom home? She's not going to survive flying just under the speed of sound for fifteen hours without a spacesuit. Speaking of which, I am damned hungry. Is anyone else hungry?"

Dad tosses me a frozen orange as hard as a rock.

"Very funny."

Mom looks up at him and 'eeps.' "What is that?"

"You don't remember me?" He bows, then shifts himself down to his human disguise.

"Oh… it's you." Mom swallows.

"Hey, wow, this is weird." I put my arms around both of them. "I've never had my parents together in the same place before ever."

"At least it's scenic," says Laniah.

"Sure, if you like miles of snow and mountains." I shiver in spite of her magic keeping me warm. Merely looking at this place is making me feel cold.

"I'll take her home." He offers her his elbow.

Mom remains rigid, terrified.

"Mom, you know how the pretty ones aren't really angels?" I ask. She glances at me.

"That means we're not really demons. He's not evil."

My mother takes in a deep breath and lets it out slow. "All right. If she trusts you, I suppose I can." She threads her arm around Dad's.

"Well, he did go to the ends of the Earth for you." I wink.

Dad smiles, and the pair of them vanish in a fiery cloud.

"Grr. I wish I could do that. He teleported, didn't he?"

Laniah pats me on the back. "You are more powerful than us in some ways, but weaker in others. Your human part anchors you in this place. It provides you strength, but prevents you from traversing the dimensions at will. You need gates."

"Right. Damn. That means another long-ass flight. Crap, I'm hungry."

She takes my hand and stretches her wings. "You will not suffer harm by not eating in the time it takes us to return home. Though, you will probably eat an entire pizza when you're back."

I narrow my eyes. "Challenge accepted."

# 23

## CIRCLES AND CHARMS

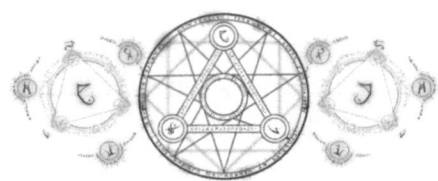

Monday, late morning, I'm flopped on my couch in a hooded sweatshirt, sweat pants, and black fuzzy slippers.

No, it's not particularly cold in here... I'm *mentally* cold from Antarctica. And it isn't like this stuff really helps. Anything under a hundred degrees feels chilly to me, and like seventy or lower is probably how humans feel when it's freezing outside. Okay, maybe I'm exaggerating a little, but in all my life, how much or how little I had on never really made any difference in feelings of warmth.

Today, though, I'm experimenting with 'warm' stuff.

And okay, Mom's visiting. I'm not about to do the nature girl thing with her here. That's only slightly less awkward than watching her kiss Dad. Not that she did... at least anywhere I saw. Probably happened the night they conceived me, but she was under a mind control enchantment. She also hasn't said much at all about what went on after the two of them disappeared other than telling me they walked 'for a while' on a stone path surrounded by 'lawns of fire' before they stepped through a portal into her living room.

Laniah's prediction didn't quite come true. I did not eat an entire pizza myself, though I most likely could have. I stopped by Mom's place to check on her and killed her stash of empanadas. Not really sure if she's visiting me because she doesn't want to be alone, is scared, or just felt like it. Random teleportation to giant labyrinths in Antarctica can leave a mark on one's psyche.

Still, I don't mind. And it gave me a chance to finally introduce her to Ashley. The kid showed up a little after nine when Tracy left for school, wearing the plain white T-shirt 'dress' she probably slept in. Of course, her favorite flying faerie toy came along, too. Natalie gave her a couple other little things, as well as a new pink heart-shaped locket. The charm's got that protection spell my friend used on her the one time Shaar'Nath attacked me in the street. Not that either of us have any reason to suspect anything, but after the warmongers grabbed Mom, better safe than sorry. And there's plenty else in this part of town that could hurt her other than idiots from another plane.

I don't envy Tracy her schedule, though. Some days, she has early classes, then goes to Starbucks to work. Other days, she works early and goes to a later class. For a couple years, the woman's not going to know what free time is. So, yeah, I don't really mind watching Ashley for her so much. Though, my mother finds it humorous someone's trusting me with their child. To hear her talk, Ashley's going to turn into a car-stealing, graffiti-writing, pot-smoking teen if left to my influence.

The kid doesn't have my weak impulse control. I'm not going to encourage her to vandalize and steal cars. Once she's like sixteen or so, if she wants to try a little weed, well… who am I to soapbox about that? The stuff's nowhere near as dangerous as alcohol. If whiskey could cure shit, I bet big pharma would make sure booze stayed illegal, too.

Anyway, Mom gushes over the kid like she's found a ten gigabyte store of kitten videos online. Of course, my mother keeps giving me the 'I really want to be a grandmother' look every so often. I'm really in no hurry. Cripes, Mom… I'm only twenty-three.

A few hours of cartoons later, Ashley hops off the couch and runs to the bathroom.

"So you and Dad…"

Mom glances at me. The look on her face could be used to replace stop signs. "I don't even know him. And he's not human. I..." She looks down and sighs. "I can't remember the night we..."

"Right. No need for those details." I grin.

"He's not in love with me. It's like John Gilbert."

I quirk an eyebrow. "Who?"

"Oh, I was maybe twenty at the time. Met him at a concert. Went home with him. We were intimate on and off that weekend then we never spoke to each other again. Nothing between us but a good time."

It's so stunning to hear my mom talk about a casual hookup all I can do is blurt, "Yet you still remember his name?"

"The sex was good." She wags her eyebrows. "*Really* good."

I squirm.

Mom laughs. "That's about the same look you gave me when you realized I wrote romance novels."

Curled in a ball, I peer over my knees at her. "Mom... you're the same woman who almost fainted when you caught me with Charlie."

"Ugh." Mom buries her face in her hand. "I still can't believe you asked me for advice. Most fourteen-year-olds caught in the act freak the hell out. It made it so much worse that you were so blasé about it."

Ashley emerges from the hallway, crosses behind the couch, and goes into the kitchen.

I giggle nervously. "Oh, I *was* embarrassed. Just didn't show it. I only asked you for advice because I wanted to flip things around and make you the one who felt like you did something wrong by walking in on us."

"Figured." Mom lets out a wistful sigh. "You were really a handful."

"And you want to go through that all over again?" I glance down at my sweatshirt-covered belly. "What kind of hellion do you think is going to come out of me? Can you picture a two-year-old hopped up on sugar literally *flying* around the room shredding the walls?"

She laughs.

The soft *whump* of my freezer closing precedes the scrape of a chair dragging, then the ka-chunk of the rune oven opening.

"Oh, she's brave," I mutter.

Mom raises an eyebrow. "What?"

"The kid's tempting the rune oven from hell. Last time I used it, a chorizo-and-egg burrito came out tasting like s'mores."

Mom cringes. "That's horrible."

"I know, right?"

"No, I mean that someone put eggs in a burrito." She goes off on a ramble about 'bastardized' Mexican food.

We both fall silent at a tiny voice chanting barely over a whisper. It kinda sounds like Latin, but no way this kid knows ancient languages. 'Course I don't know Latin either so I've got no idea if she's making words up.

"That's unusual," whispers Mom.

"Yeah."

I stand and sneak into the kitchen, Mom right behind me.

One of the kitchen chairs sits up against the cabinets. Ashley's standing on the counter in front of the rune oven, holding a squeeze bottle of ketchup, the bright light inside the infernal machine painting a clear outline of her scrawny body in shadow on her shirt. A book I don't remember seeing before lays open on the counter by her feet.

Mom and I edge up behind her, amused and curious.

The kid's drawn a circle of ketchup around a frozen hamburger inside the oven, adding little squiggles here and there like runes around the outside.

"What are you doing?" I ask.

Ashley points with her toe at a book open on the counter with a diagram of a similar pattern labeled 'Circle of Power.'

"Is that real?" I ask.

Mom slips past me and brushes her hand down the page. "It sure looks like it. This appears to be a protective ward against demonic energy."

"Yep." Ashley nods. "I'm warding my lunch against another daemon."

"*Another* daemon?" asks Mom.

The child leans into the oven long enough to add two more

squiggles, then sets the ketchup down and closes the door. "Last time Brook made me a pot pie, a little daemon crawled out of it and tried to eat me."

Mom blinks. "Maybe you should get a new rune oven."

Ashley goes wide-eyed at her, then faces me with her arms thrust out to either side. "*See!* I'm telling you. Listen to your mom."

Both Mom and I laugh.

The kid hits the orange button on the oven before leaping at me like she's diving away from a live hand grenade. I catch her and back up a few steps.

Mom stays by the counter paging through the book. "Where did you get this book, sweetie? This is pretty advanced."

"Liberry."

I mouth 'library' in time with Mom correcting her.

"You're a mage?" asks Ashley.

"Ehh, sort of." Mom grins. "I've got a little talent, but mostly in divination."

A weird purple flash flickers inside the rune oven for a few seconds before the 'food's done' chime sounds.

Mom opens the door and the quite normal smell of a cooked cheeseburger—tinged with ketchup—fills the kitchen. "Looks fine."

I blink. Did the kid actually do magic or is this total coincidence. Sometimes my oven *does* work normally. That's the most frustrating part, the utter randomness with which it invokes the spirits of chaos.

We relocate to the couch and watch a kid's movie, something about a plucky teenage mermaid leading a peasant revolt against a corrupt monarchy. Mom spends more time reading over that magic book than looking at the screen. After the past few days, I'm more than happy to give my brain a rest and let it operate at the level of a story meant for children.

Evidently, Ashley's seen this one already. I can tell because she sings along with most of the musical numbers.

A little after three, the doorbell rings.

I get up to answer, half expecting more crap of the supernatural persuasion, but it's only Tracy… though she's shivering and looks out of sorts.

"Hey, c'mon in. You okay?"

She scurries past me. "Yeah. I'm just… wow."

"Hi, Mom," says Ashley without looking back. "Movie's almost over. Can we stay a few minutes?"

"Sure, hon." Tracy paces around, still shrouded in the chill of having recently been outside. "Wow, it's a bit warm in here."

"Sorry. Got the heat cranked."

Ashley holds her arm up, pointing at the ceiling. "She *always* has the heat cranked. Hello? Demon?"

"So, what's got you shaking?" I ask. "You have a near miss with the cops or something? If they haven't shown up about the pawn shop thing yet, they won't."

"No, it's not that." She breathes into her hands a few times trying to warm them. "I got called to the office at the school today. They told me I'd been randomly selected for this program to help low income students. Basically gave me a full scholarship as long as I can keep my grades up. It even covers books and supplies. I had no idea they even did anything like that."

"That's awesome," I say with perhaps unconvincing surprise.

Tracy stares at me. "You…?"

I smile, shrugging one shoulder. "You just have to know how to ask."

"*You* did that?!" Tracy grabs my hand. "You charmed someone?"

Mom clucks her tongue in disapproval like I'd eaten cookies before dinner.

"No, of course not. I merely pointed out the specifics of your situation. The school had funds set aside for helping people in certain situations…" I examine my fingernails.

"You shouldn't mind control people," says Mom. "It's rude."

Ashley stands on the sofa and points at me. "Bad minion."

Mom laughs.

I stick my tongue out at the kid. She responds in kind.

"No, I didn't *mind control* anyone. Don't think I'm even able to do that... I'm just really charming when I need to be." I wink.

Ashley grins, spins around, and flops back down to watch the last ten or so minutes of the movie.

Tracy hugs me and bursts into tears. When she calms enough, she whispers, "I won't tell anyone."

"Cool."

She lets out a long, slow exhale. "Holy shit... it feels like I won the lottery."

"Now only if you could use that charming personality of yours on those foolish creatures," says Mom.

I fold my arms and glance into my kitchen. "If I destroy the world, it's not going to be because of some Pillar of Creation... it'll happen because I hit the wrong button on that rune oven."

"Get. A. New. One," yells Ashley. "Cooking dinner should not require sorcery to avoid death!"

Laughing, I collapse on the couch between my Mom and the kid. Tracy flops to Ashley's right.

For the next oh, fifteen minutes, the biggest problem in my world is how a mermaid revolution ends.

*fin*

## ACKNOWLEDGMENTS

Thank you for reading *The Gate to Oblivion*!
Additional thanks to Alexandria Thompson for the cover art.

# ABOUT THE AUTHOR

Originally from South Amboy NJ, Matthew has been creating science fiction and fantasy worlds for most of his reasoning life. Since 1996, he has developed the "Divergent Fates" world, in which *Division Zero, Virtual Immortality, The Awakened Series, The Harmony Paradox, and the Daughter of Mars series* take place. Along with being an editor at Curiosity Quills press, he has worked in IT and technical support.

Matthew is an avid gamer, a recovered WoW addict, Gamemaster for two custom RPG systems, and a fan of anime, British humour, and intellectual science fiction that questions the nature of reality, life, and what happens after it.

He is also fond of cats.

Visit me online at:
Facebook: https://www.facebook.com/MatthewSCoxAuthor
Amazon: https://www.amazon.com/author/mscox
Pinterest: https://www.pinterest.com/matthewcox10420/
Goodreads: https://www.goodreads.com/author/show/7712730.Matthew_S_Cox
Email: mcox2112@gmail.com

# OTHER BOOKS BY MATTHEW S. COX

Divergent Fates Universe Novels

Division Zero series

- Division Zero
- Lex De Mortuis
- Thrall
- Guardian

The Awakened series

- Prophet of the Badlands
- Archon's Queen
- Grey Ronin
- Daughter of Ash
- Zero Rogue
- Angel Descended

Daughter of Mars series

- The Hand of Raziel
- Araphel
- Ghost Black

Virtual Immortality series

- Virtual Immortality
- The Harmony Paradox

Divergent Fates Anthology

(Fiction Novels - Adult)

The Roadhouse Chronicles Series

- One More Run
- The Redeemed
- Dead Man's Number

Faded Skies series

- Heir Ascendant
- Ascendant Unrest
- Ascendant Revolution

Temporal Armistice Series

- Nascent Shadow
- The Shadow Collector

Vampire Innocent series

- A Nighttime of Forever
- A Beginner's Guide to Fangs
- The Artist of Ruin
- The Last Family Road Trip

Standalones

- Wayfarer: AV494
- Axillon99
- Chiaroscuro: The Mouse and the Candle
- The Far Side of Promise anthology
- Operation: Chimera (with Tony Healey)
- The Dysfunctional Conspiracy (with Christopher Veltmann)

Winter Solstice series (with J.R. Rain)

- Convergence
- Containment

Alexis Silver series (with J.R. Rain)

- Silver Light
- Deep Silver

Samantha Moon Origins series (with J.R. Rain)

- New Moon Rising
- Moon Mourning

Maddy Wimsey series (with J.R. Rain)

- The Devil's Eye
- The Drifting Gloom

Samantha Moon Case Files series (with J.R. Rain)

- Blood Moon
- Dead Moon

Young Adult Novels

- Caller 107
- The Summer the World Ended
- Nine Candles of Deepest Black
- The Eldritch Heart
- The Forest Beyond the Earth
- Out of Sight

Middle Grade Novels

Tales of Widowswood series

- Emma and the Banderwigh
- Emma and the Silk Thieves
- Emma and the Silverbell Faeries
- Emma and the Elixir of Madness
- Emma and the Weeping Spirit

Standalones

- Citadel: The Concordant Sequence
- The Cursed Codex
- The Menagerie of Jenkins Bailey
- Sophie's Light